T0079725

Karolinum Press

ABOUT THE AUTHOR

Jan Procházka (1929–1971) was a Czech screenwriter and novelist. Many of his novels were inspired by or written concurrently with his screenplays. Born into a farming family in south Moravia, he studied agriculture before rising up the ranks of the Communist Party. He was the head of a youth farm, worked for the Central Committee of the Czechoslovak Youth Union, and was then a member of the Central Committee for the Czech Communist Party. He began his artistic career in 1956 with his first novel, and then in 1959 became a screenwriter for Czechoslovakia's famous Barrandov Film Studios. He even became a close associate of the Communist President, Antonín Novotný during this time. In the 1960s Procházka was a leading figure in the reformist wing of the Communist Party, publishing in newspapers and revues and pointing out the failures of the regime. With the Soviet led invasion of Czechoslovakia in 1968, he was declared a *persona non grata*, his work was banned, and he became the victim of a vicious smear campaign by the secret police who edited together tapped phone-lines to ruin his reputation. Today he is most famous as the writer behind the brilliant – and instantly banned – 1969 new wave film *Ucho* (The Ear), and other screenplays for the director Karel Kachyňa (*Kočár do Vídně*, *Noc nevěsty*). *Ucho* has been adapted into a TV play (1983 ZDF, ORF) by Pavel Kohout and another movie *Noc bezMoci* (2015) by Ivan Trajkov.

MODERN CZECH CLASSICS

Jan Procházka
Ear

Translation from the Czech by Mark Corner

Afterword by David Vaughan

KAROLINUM PRESS 2022

KAROLINUM PRESS is a publishing department
of Charles University
Ovocný trh 3–5, 116 36 Prague 1, Czech Republic
www.karolinum.cz

Cover and graphic design by Zdeněk Ziegler
Set and printed in the Czech Republic by Karolinum Press
First English edition

Cataloging-in Publication Data is available
from the National Library of the Czech Republic

ISBN 978-80-246-5135-4 (pbk)
ISBN 978-80-246-5136-1 (pdf)
ISBN 978-80-246-5319-8 (epub)
ISBN 978-80-246-5320-4 (mobi)

1

Anna gets out of the car in her stockings and steps onto a damp pavement at night. Her shoes felt too tight, so she's holding them in her hands. Her bag is slung over her shoulder. She is dressed in a long evening gown looking like a sack. She has a fox fur round her neck and uses a bare elbow to press a crumpled shiny raincoat against her waist. She is singing a Slovak song. Whenever she's tipsy, she takes to singing.

'Put your shoes on,' he says. His mild tone is almost soothing. Which is not quite how he's feeling.

'Don't speak to me!' Irritation courses through her at every word he speaks. 'Be so kind as to leave me in peace. Got that?'

She turns away from him to the car.

'Wherever did I put that hat of mine?'

She is all affability talking to the chauffeur. 'You can't leave me here all hatless, Vlad.'

She always addresses chauffeurs as if they're part of the family.

She has been kneeling on the edge of the back seat with her head back inside the car. Broad calves lead to ankles spread wide. These stay on the street. Bending forward amplifies her figure. Ludvík turns away. Moves at speed across the pavement. Takes a good look around. But they are the only ones in the street. Two rows of trees grow along the pavement. Shiny in the trunk. Maybe beech.

He is now standing in front of the gate of the little villa. He tries the handle. Finds it locked.

He realises that he knew all along it would be locked. Feels in a trouser pocket. Then in the other pocket. Then with both hands at once in his two jacket pockets. Removes the raincoat draped over his shoulder, holds it in one hand and feels in it with the other.

'Could you get the keys from your handbag?'

'Sod off,' she replies. Without so much as throwing him a glance. She lays out the cape, handbag, shoes and a bouquet of roses on the garden wall. She has a paper hat back on her head now.

The car drives off. It fades into the distance at great speed.

'You locked it.' He heaves a sigh. 'You were the last to leave the house. I was already sitting in the car when you came out.'

'That's your problem. You know what your problem is…? The beastly way you behave! Going out of the house first before me! Leaving me to follow in your wake like a dog! Is that something to brag about?'

All the same she opens her handbag. And rummages inside.

'I haven't got them. I know what's in there and what isn't. I haven't lost my wits yet.'

About fifty yards away a black limousine is hugging the kerb. It seems to have appeared in the street without a sound.

It has switched off its sidelights. A standard issue government limousine. Just like the car that brought them. No one gets out of it.

Ludvík notices the limousine.

'You were wearing a cape. You must have put them in its pocket.'

He is talking to empty air.

Anna is loafing around on the edge of the pavement in her stockings. No one can mistake what she's up to. Something a woman has to pull up her skirt to do.

'Have you gone mad...?' he hisses at her. 'There's people over there.'

She has pulled up the long skirt to mid-thigh.

'You mean that car...? The one with the lights out? Who would be there...? Who would sit in a car without any lights on?'

The car has suddenly begun to back away. Without putting the headlights on. A tyre can be heard scraping against the kerb.

Anna stops what she's doing.

Lowers her dress. Turns round.

'Do you think they were playing away from home?'

Just her style of question.

2

The officer is wearing white gloves.

He opens the car door for them.

He salutes.

Ludvík greets him formally with 'Hail to labour!'

In her long skirt Anna emerges very awkwardly. In the event she has to hold it up. Her handbag falls to the ground. 'If one green bottle should accidentally fall...' She laughs as she sings. Without a moment's hesitation the officer hands over the bag.

He gives Ludvík a parking permit.

'One one seven', he informs him.

He gives the same number to Jindřich. Jindřich has driven them over.

'Have a good time!' He gives them a nod from the car.

They are already on their way up...

By way of the marble staircase...

Along the expensive carpet...

Between pots of ivy. And flunkies on guard.

'None of your come here, go there, stay in line, no more wine,' Anna is saying. Out loud. 'Understood? I'm not your little fool. Ready to be shouted at all evening.'

'Don't you know how to speak quietly?' he asks.

Doormen in livery open the dazzling white and gilded doors in front of them...

3

Anna is going through the pocket of the cape.

'An orange!' she says and gives a snort. 'I pinched one!'

She's standing on one leg. With the instep of the other she's rubbing her calf.

'How is it that I don't have those keys...?'

'How would I know.'

'Today of all days you could stop being so down in the mouth. Agreed? Today of all days! When you've got a moment, why don't you look at the calendar!'

'At the calendar.... Why at the calendar?'

'If you look at the calendar, the penny might drop. For a huge brain like yours.'

She has given up the search.

'I don't have them. Are we just going to stand around? Shall we sleep out here? Or are you going to do something? We've got a bell, haven't we?'

She presses the doorbell.

She listens. If it works, somebody should be able to hear it.

There is no sound.

'It's not working...?'

She turns to Ludvík.

'I need to take a leak. Or I'll wet myself.'

He starts to shimmy up the wall.

'For all I care... fill your pants if you must...!'

'You don't need to spell it out for me! Really, you don't need to spell it out at all. I know you don't give a damn about what I do. I've known that long enough! You don't care a fig about me! I'm not too soft in the head to know that!'

He hauls himself over the top.

Still adroit, he is already standing on the small roof over the gate and breathing heavily from exertion.

'How could you spend the whole evening talking to that Cejnar? When you say yourself that he's a fathead. Any idiot will do for your idle chatter, but you obviously can't spare a moment for me. You couldn't care less that I had to stand around abandoned for hours...'

4

The glow from the chandeliers falls on everything like a sprinkling of flour. He passes by a Venetian mirror. In the glass surface he looks sick and swollen. Red around the eyes. Someone he knows appears in the mirror.

'I'm looking for Anna.' He has to say something.

Then he sees Anna. Just where he's heading. Standing with a bunch of women. All wearing paper hats. They've put numbers on them with lipstick. They're laughing about it.

He swings round at once.

So she won't catch sight of him.

A bit further on he repeats the lie to someone else: 'I'm looking for Anna.'

He launches himself and drops down from the wall into the garden with a thud, his hands landing on the lawn.

He's landed in a molehill or worse. It's all over the palms of his hands. He wipes them on the grass.

Anna hears his steps in the garden.

As he moves away.

'Wake up, Ludi!' She calls out to Ludvík. 'The other set's hanging in the kitchen.'

She takes out a handkerchief. Blows her nose. Moves away from the gate.

Goes to the wall. Puts on her cape. Takes her things which are falling onto the pavement. Gathers a slapdash bundle into her arms.

Now that she's alone, tiredness has caught up with her.

The empty street is uninviting.

From the house comes the sound of Ludvík whistling. The same warble over and over again. A muffled call.

There's the sound of a pebble against glass.

'Go on, break the window!' She is speaking in an undertone.

She goes back to the gate.

More out of embarrassment than anything else, she tries the handle.

The gate opens!

Anna is not surprised.

'We are all idiots,' she says. 'Only you are a genius!'

She uses her knee to close the gate.

From the inside.

And tries to bolt it. With her elbow.

Finally, she manages it.

She has laid all her things on a little cement pathway running between the flowerbeds. Bending forward, she takes a cigarette out of her bag. Then a lighter. She tries to get a flame from the lighter. Gives it a shake. With her head by her knees, not realising the awkwardness of her position. Spits at it three times. For luck. This time a real flame flares up. For a moment Anna's face is lit up by its glow. The open pores of her bad skin. Which come to any blonde of a certain age. Visible traces of powder round the nose and eyes.

She straightens up. Inhales smoke greedily.

'Ludvík!' She calls to the house. Her fit of pique has passed. 'The window of the laundry room might be open.'

He jumps. The window is high above the ground. His hand has slipped off the ledge.

There's shrubbery and lots of twigs by the wall. Ludvík is fighting his way through the undergrowth in the darkness. Anna is calling the lad from the other side of the house.

'Ludi!'

'Sleeping like a log,' says Ludvík. Sounding furious.

He keeps trying. Manages to get a hold. With both hands. Succeeds in putting his weight on his knees. It's hard work. He's in his best trousers and they're tight. He bangs his head on the top of the window-frame. For a split second it looks like he'll lose his grip and fall back into the shrubbery. But he's managed to get his trunk across the window-sill. For a moment he relaxes in this position.

Anna arrives. She's come crashing through the undergrowth. Stands in front of Ludvík.

'Why did you have to climb over the gate? It wasn't locked.'

He turns his head.

'Can't you get rid of the fancy dress?'

He's referring to her paper hat.

'You're looking at me? That's something for the record books...'

'What's unlocked?'

'I don't know what it's called. It's metal, is commonly found in the fence, you use it to get from the street into the garden...'

Anna's mood is unchanged.

'Bullshit!'

'You haven't spoken like that here in a long time. Makes me wonder what I've been missing. How else could I have got here? Over the fence? Me? In this skirt...? Use your head,' she says.

'You don't have to be the only one using language like that,' she continues. 'You could be on the receiving end of it.'

He slithers forward heading indoors. Pressing sore knees against the window ledge.

Anna talks without removing the cigarette from her mouth. She's looking between the trees. At the villa next door. Its lights are on.

'Klepáč arrived from Moscow the day before yesterday. Their blinds were down till today. They haven't even been at the reception. He's been away for a month but when he comes back the Klepáč woman knows that she has a real man there.'

He slides further in.

Grabs hold of something inside.

'I've got washing hanging up. Don't break the clothes line.'

He's just broken it.

'Wouldn't think of it,' he says.

His body is off balance. He can't avoid what's happening.

He's fallen over.

Something inside collapses with a clatter.

It takes him a while to find his bearings.

Lying among pots and rags. In a pile of spilt washing-powder. Surrounded by specimens of Anna's underwear.

7

'When there is freezing...you understand? Freezing...?'

'Yes, yes,' he hears himself say in Russian. 'I say only a little, but I understand everything.'

'That's good.' The general is pleased.

The mixed party of Czechs and Russians have glasses in their hands. A Czechoslovak major is obligingly replacing a Soviet general's empty glass. With a full one. A Baroque majolica stove stands behind them. A huge painting by Brožík dominates the wallpaper.

'How nicely they offer us their welcome,' a young woman says.

She's a member of the general's party.

'We receive such hospitality in Brno. In Bratislava, and in Closetse...!'

'Košice,' one of the Czech women corrected her.

'A dreadfully nice reception...'

The woman makes the general a little nervous. He turns to face Ludvík.

'When the frost lies heavy...! Comrade Deputy minister!'

His forehead juts out in front of a shiny skull. 'I mean when it's twenty, thirty degrees below...'

He takes a drink. All at once the glass is empty.

'Can you still lay foundations...?'

'He is asking whether we can use cement in frost,' the major translates for Ludvík.

'I can follow him,' says Ludvík. 'Of course I know what he's saying.'

The waiter replaces the general's empty goblet.

The Russian raises his eyebrows.

'What a people!' he says. 'They never give a soldier any respite here.'

'When there's a frost,' Ludvík searches for the right words 'we cannot fabricate in this country.'

'It's not possible to lay foundations in a frost,' says the major, finding other words.

'Oh!' The general expresses his surprise with a sigh. 'That is unfortunate.'

'Iglava'. The Russian woman is still trying to count off Czech towns. 'Pilzena'.

'Plzeň!' the general suggests to her. 'Beer!' he adds with a laugh. Everyone has joined in the laughter.

'We can lay foundations in a frost! You should come and see them! Take a tour! And you are from...?'

'From Mohelnice.'

'Mogelnice', says the Czechoslovak major. 'Our 'h' is a 'g' in Russian. It's a what do you call it, administrative district, the Gana – Hana – area', explains the major to the general. 'Mogelnice the townlet is part of it. Mogelnice is a kind of town, isn't it?'

'It's a town,' says Ludvík.

'Who cares anyway'.

'You must come and visit us,' the general repeats. 'You absolutely must.'

He's looking at the stucco ceiling.

As if his mind is elsewhere.

'You haven't appointed a minister for the building industry?'

'Yes, we have,' says Ludvík. 'Why wouldn't we have one? The comrade minister is Košara.'

The general raises his eyebrows.

'But our people have informed me there is a vacancy at the moment...!' he says, looking surprised.

'He should be right here,' says Ludvík as he looks around. 'He must be somewhere.'

'He's sent his apologies,' says a young man.

This is the first time the young man has opened his mouth.

Ludvík doesn't know who he is.

'What do you mean, he's sent his apologies?'

The young man is already on the way out.

'Let's have a toast!' says the general. 'In the way soldiers do.'

He raises his voice. Tries to find the right words. 'In the way Czechs do!' he bawls.

The young Russian woman squeals with enthusiasm and claps.

'Face about...! Arms present...!' He is proud of having remembered the words in Czech. Clinks glasses with Ludvík. With gusto. Wine gets splashed. Fortunately, it's white wine.

8

He knows where the switch is. Shuffles over to it. Turns the switch. Still in the dark.

'Someone's blown the fuses again.'

Anna is standing outside. In front of the open window.

'I'm curious whether you said something to him. He took a coil from the radio. Did he say anything to you about taking a radio coil?'

'Well...something like that.'

'Stop lying! When did he mention it to you? When? When you last saw him? That was a week ago. If anyone spoils him, it's you.'

Ludvk has already opened the door.

Onto a narrow staircase.

He feels for the wall with his hand and goes upstairs. In darkness.

Leaves the door wide open.

Fingers touch against another switch. He turns it. But still no light comes on.

'The little scoundrel,' he says.

There's another switch in the hall.

Ludvk tries this switch too. Just as useless.

He fumbles in his pockets. Pulls out a lighter. Having got hold of the lighter, he finds cigarettes. First of all he lights one.

Keeps the lighter on. Carries the small flame over to an alcove...

Where the fuses are.

Moves the light from one fuse to another.

Tightens them with his free hand. But none of them seems to be loose.

No fuses blown. He unscrews one all the same.

Examines the wires. Nothing wrong with the fuse.

Goes once again to turn the switch.

In the kitchen. Nothing.

The glow from his lighter is the only relief from the darkness.

He bumps his leg against a chair.

Reaches the row of pegs. There's a shoehorn hanging there. A bottle opener. Some rubber bands for sealing preserves. No keys hanging anywhere.

'It's a mess wherever you look,' he says. 'You can't find something that isn't here to begin with.'

He opens a drawer. Cutlery inside. And a leftover bit of candle. He lights the candle. Puts it on the table. Clicks shut the lighter and returns it to his pocket.

Another pebble strikes the window.

He hears Anna calling from outside:

'Is it going to take you till morning?'

Fortunately, she sounds far away.

He has gone back into the hall.

'The keys aren't anywhere,' he says. He has an inkling that Anna is standing behind the door.

'How would I know where they are?'

'They're hanging on the peg.'

'Are they bugger.'

'Where else would they be hanging?'

'How would I know?'

He is by the door now.

He sees that the keys are in the lock! On the inside!

He can't get his head round this.

He tries the doorknob.

It's not locked!

It opens.

He stands in amazement face to face with Anna. The eternal paper hat is still on her head.

'How can it be unlocked...? When I tried it a moment ago it was locked.'

'Just like the gate, isn't it! For goodness' sake! Don't you know how to do up your laces?' Anna's in a bad temper. She feels cold.

She tries the switch.

'What have you done now? I thought you were repairing the fuses?'

'There's nothing wrong with the fuses. The electricity is down.'

Ludvk shuts the door. And turns the key.

He's been thinking things over.

'But didn't you lock it earlier? I saw you locking it...! And the keys are on the inside.'

'When we're out of the house he does what he wants. Haven't I always told you so? The boys come and whistle for him. Who knows where he's been? Who knows whether they were all in our house!'

'All the same would he have left the key in the lock? Wouldn't he have removed the key when he'd locked up? And hung it up, so that we'd know nothing about what he'd been doing...!'

'So we had a visitation by the Holy Spirit. Give the lad a smack or two in the morning. Then perhaps he'll let you know what's been going on. He's been waiting for a good hiding for long enough.'

Anna gives a yawn.

Her memory tells her how to get to the kitchen. A dim light is coming through the windows. She heads for the fridge.

She takes out a bottle of vodka. Uncorks it. Takes a swig.

Ludvík is already in the kitchen.

'Come off it,' he says, 'Don't drink vodka from the bottle. You know who drinks vodka from the bottle...?'

'I know all right.'

'Can't you take a glass?'

'I was born in a pub, dummy! You should be used to that by now! Our Comrade President is another one who drinks straight from the bottle!'

Ludvík goes and shuts the door between the kitchen and the hall.

'Sorry,' says Anna, 'I forgot that the comrades never sleep! The comrades spend all their time listening!'

She stands the bottle on the fridge. 'All the meat in my fridge will be rotten by morning', he says.

Ludvík finds a candle and lights it. He takes a small plate, turns it upside down and lets a little wax drip onto the bottom. He attaches the candle to the plate.

He examines the keys in his hand.

'They're my keys all right,' he says. He recognises the key ring.

'There you are,' says Anna. 'And still you keep arguing! Your keys were hanging on the peg in the kitchen. Here!' She shows him where. 'I locked up with mine...'

'I'll have words with him! If he's had people over, I'll get even with him.'

Anna takes the meat out of the fridge.

'Where should I put the meat? Outside the window? But it's warm outside,' observes Anna. 'You could take it into the cellar, couldn't you? Put the dish on the floor in the cellar.'

She removes a porcelain dish full of meat from the fridge.

Sniffs at it.

Touches it.

'The meat's quite cold!' she says. 'They must have cut the electricity just a short while ago.'

But at that moment she looks up.

Looks once again at the neighbour's house. The one she's already been looking at from the garden.

'There's lights on next door. Klepáč has his lights on. How come they only cut off the supply to our place?'

'Maybe a fuse has blown on the power pole outside,' he says. He too is looking through the window. Trying to see something between the trees. He stands there a while. Turns back. Faces the kitchen dresser.

'Where do you keep the torch?' Ludvk roots about in the dresser. 'Is any of this stuff where it should be?' He's on edge.

'Of course it is. What matters is in the right place. What about you? I wouldn't say the same thing about you!'

Anna goes to the dresser. Uses her body to push Ludvk to one side. There's reason behind her roughness. She's hitching up her dress and squatting down. Pulls out the bottom drawer. Passes him the torch. Passes it so that she lights up his face. Takes the chance to blow on his cheek from close quarters.

'It's a long time since I dazzled you!' she says. 'Much too long.'

'Leave off!' says Ludvk. 'I've enough to worry about without your stupidities.'

9

He is forcing his way between bellies and backs.

At last he spots his target, Pučák.

By a marble table. Chewing. And swallowing.

The table is bursting with used china dishes and unfinished glasses. Ashtrays overflowing.

A group of coal-miners in folk costume are singing loudly nearby.

'They've had their snouts nicely in the trough!' says Pučák.

He surveys the workers with a look of kindly understanding, as if he's watching children.

'They've pulled out all the stops.'

'What happened at the cabinet meeting?' Ludvík hears the cracking in his own voice.

'Did you get to our...report?'

Pučák is apparently not listening. He is on a scanning tour, looking in all directions. Finally, he re-directs his gaze to Ludvík.

'Not eating?' he says.

'Not hungry.'

He lights a cigarette.

'It's what the people think today that counts,' says a voice from somewhere right behind their backs. 'The people are still developing. Our people are still on the way forward. It is of no concern to me whether someone is a Catholic or a Moslem. All that matters to me is whether they accept or do not accept our socialist aims.'

'Exactly so.' Pučák turns round. 'Indeed.'

'Is this true, Comrade Minister? Or is it not so?'

'It is one hundred per cent correct.'

The skinny fellow looks pleased at this. He looks like a visionary on a mission. A forelock has taken a dive onto his forehead. The soft collar of his shirt is crumpled. Even the knot of his tie participates in the untidiness. He resembles

a revolutionary poet. 'I came right to the workshop floor to have a look at Mareček.' He is now speaking only to the minister. 'He had a picture of the Virgin Mary on his machine. Next to a badge of honour for specially productive workers...! The party chairman says: 'I don't know what to do about this...' I say to him: 'Let your mind be broad! Did we prevail in the revolution or did we not prevail...? Judge the person according to this: does he accept or not accept our socialist aims?'

'Let him pray,' says the minister. He raises his eyebrows. He has a face that is red and fat. 'Let Mareček say his prayers as he wants,' he goes on. 'If it helps him. We will not give this a mention in the newspapers...will we? But we won't go apeshit about it either...!'

'I am so glad, Comrade Minister, that you have the same opinion as I do,' says the fellow. 'I am pleased.'

Pučák shakes his hand.

Finds it stuck in his enthusiastic grip for a while.

Pučák has already turned. To face Ludvík:

'It's only Tuesday', he says. 'Has it become Thursday already? The government meets on Thursday.'

'But they summoned Košara. To the government meeting...' says Ludvík. He blinks nervously. 'They telephoned from you... From the presidium. So that he'd rush headlong to see them...'

Pučák looks round.

Then he looks up. Suspiciously. Overhead they have a chandelier with a modernist design. Symmetrical brass plates hanging down. Their shape is special. It even makes them look like ears.

'Move along a bit,' says the minister. 'I don't like standing... under....under...'

They advance a few steps.

They advance until they're behind a polished chest-of-drawers. Until they're by the window. Now they're standing behind a rubber plant. They might as well be in a bush.

Pučák lowers his voice. 'You don't know what's happened to Košara?'

Pučák gives Ludvík a quick glance.

'So they didn't talk...at all... to you?'

'Who....?'

'I'm sorry,' says the minister. He is suddenly unsure of himself. Puts down his plate on the chest. Apologises. Hastily. 'I have the president of the Parliament here...I must remind him of... Oldřich!' he calls out to someone. 'Olda!' And he goes right up to some tall man. Meanwhile the coal-miners are tossing someone up in the air.

'Look at how clumsily they handle a fork! And a spoon! Look – see for yourself.'

Cejnar is whispering into his ear.

They are standing next to a long table groaning under platters full of food. One waiter actually manages to drop a slice of ham into the salad.

'Not one of them is a tray trotter. Not a single one. Undercover cops – nothing but.'

He nudges Ludvík with his elbow.

'A slice of salmon,' he says out loud. To a waiter.

The waiter surveys the trays of food.

'Salmon is the pink stuff', says Cejnar.

'They've taken him in,' he then says to Ludvík.

They are by the door between two grand rooms, which is the quietest place to be.

Cejnar has the yellow face of a heavy smoker. Feverish little eyes. Never stops looking around.

'They also took Tondl, Klepáč and Šlesingr.'

'Why... I ask you... Košara...?'

'Košara's name used to be Jewish. Karpeles, wasn't it?'

Ludvík is silent for a while.

'Košara would do nothing of his own accord. He'd take no step on his own – even across his own kitchen. Take the report on the brickworks. We practically had to kick him into seeing it our way.'

'If I was in your shoes, I wouldn't shout that from the rooftops right now.'

Music takes over the room.

They start to dance. The Czech Beseda salon dance. The women have the miners' paper hats on their heads, while the men wear the women's scarves like turbans. Everyone is applauding them, following the beat. A merry time is had by all...

'The main thing is to have nothing on paper!' says Cejnar. 'Flush anything on paper down the loo. No written record. That's the way you could get tangled up in this!'

'Why me?' he says. 'Tell me why it should be me.'

'I mean, just in case. Just in case. To deal with all eventualities.' Cejnar takes a cognac off the waiter's tray. Downs it in one. 'One moment!' he says. Helps himself to another glass. 'To meeting the plan by exceeding it.'

'The mayonnaise is always stale here,' whispers a woman passer-by. To another woman. 'It was stale last time too. If the mayo has those yellow bits on it, it's stale!'

She spots Ludvík. Looks up in surprise.

'Anna's trying to find you,' she says. Points to a room full of noise. 'She's at the other end...'

'Yes,' says Ludvík.

The other woman is attractive. And young. With long earrings in her lobes. And a black fur spreading its lustre around her neck.

It does not go unnoticed by Ludvík.

Despite the anxiety his situation brings him...

The steps down to the cellar are narrow. The ceiling is low.

Ludvík makes his descent practically stooping. The torch is in one hand, the dish of meat in the other. He has to step over jars. Over plates and pans which clog up the stairway.

'You could at least wash the dishes sometimes,' he says.

'Sometime – that's when I'll do it,' replies Anna from the kitchen.

In the cellar he finds shallow trays and crates of fruit. A large crate full of potatoes. But above all a lot of empty bottles. He puts the meat onto a wooden plank that's lying around.

'Don't put meat on the plank,' calls Anna from up above. 'Put it on the concrete.'

'Whatever you say!'

He transfers the dish to the cement.

Straightens himself up.

And suddenly notices the door opposite.

Leading from the cellar to the garden.

It's not shut!

It's ajar.

Ludvík squeezes his way through the junk to reach it.

'I'll give that boy such a hiding!' he says.

Shuts the door. Bolts it.

Points the torch at a pile of cardboard boxes. Several of them are tied up with string. Starts to inspect them. Has a rummage. Flings some to one side in order to get at the ones beneath. Parks the battery on a pyramid of fruit crates in order to free his hand. Some boxes are full of empty jars for preserves. Others contain parcels of magazines tied with string.

Anna is standing on the stairs. She no longer sports her paper hat. In her hand is a metal candlestick.

With a candle.

'Where are you...?' she inquires. 'What are you doing down there? I'm running a bath. The boiler's full of hot water. They must have cut the lecky just a moment ago. What are you doing with those boxes?'

'Do you remember where we put all my stuff back then? The papers? And the books?' says Ludvík. 'Those black exercise books? The ones I ... made notes in?'

There's a moment's silence from Anna.

'Just what do you look like? Don't you realise this place is full of dirt?' She goes right down into the cellar. 'What do you need your notes for right now?'

'We tied them up with string. And put them all together somewhere. I wrote them while I was at the secretariat. Once I read them to you in bed. Do you remember?'

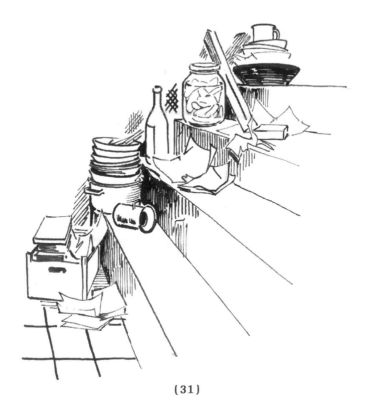

'You're always reading to me in bed. It's the main thing you do for me in bed. How could I remember it all? We've spent almost half a year reading about brickworks.' There's a note of contempt in her voice. 'I know about every brick-work in the republic.'

She takes the torch from him.

Switches it off to make a point.

'There'll be no reading tonight.' She makes a categorical statement. 'Life is not just theory. Life is also practice. At least once a week. Be the result ever so weak.'

She goes back.

Up the stairs.

'Don't tread in the pudding as you go up.'

'Leave me the torch,' says a furious Ludvík.

All of a sudden it's pitch black where he's standing.

Left helpless holding a box in his hands.

Anna puts the candlestick on a small table. In the hall. Next to the telephone. Right under the wooden staircase. She is holding the receiver to her ear.

'Why doesn't the 'phone work?' she asks. She presses the button on the cradle and dials again. 'The 'phone should still be working, shouldn't it? Even without electricity. If a government telephone doesn't work, what is there left that does?'

'Who are you ... for Christ's sake, who are you 'phoning this time...?'

Ludvík emerges from the cellar. He holds his grimy hands away from his body. He walks close to Anna. She steps forward so he has to touch her body.

'What's it matter to you who I'm calling?'

He gives an involuntary sigh.

'Stop that sighing.' Anna swings round to face him before trying the phone once more. 'I don't want any more of your sighs. They really get on my nerves. You don't have to sigh all over me. I'm calling a man, if it happens to interest you.'

'It doesn't.'

Ludvík is already in the kitchen. Washing his hands under the tap.

Speaks from above the sink. 'Didn't we put those things into my old suitcase? The brown one? With those slats around it? The one I had when I was still in Brno at the technical college?'

'I got rid of that a long time ago.'

'That's typical of you.'

'There was nothing in it! I never threw away anything else of yours. And I didn't lose anything either. Everything you've lost you've managed to lose of your own accord. The only thing you've lost with me is your virginity.'

Ludvík wants to dry his hands. A towel is hanging on one of the pegs. Next to it is a dishcloth.

The flickering flame from the candle stuck to the plate illuminates the kitchen.

He is drying his hands on the towel. Pauses all of a sudden. Sniffs at his hands. Then the towel. Then the dishcloth. Clearly the same everywhere. Another quick handwash. Dries them on a handkerchief which he pulls out of his pocket. 'The towel is for hands, the cloth is for dishes,' he says. 'I'll write it up on the wall for you one day!'

Anna comes into the kitchen with the fox fur still enwrapping her. She discards it onto a chair. She has left the candlestick and candle behind her in the hall.

'Hungry?'

'If you can chuck out an empty suitcase, you should be able to remember where you put what was in it.'

'I don't,' she says. 'But I can remember what happened ten years ago.'

'What was that?'

'That's the point. You still don't remember.'

She goes into the pantry. Flashes the torch across the shelves.

Reaches for a plate with slices of roast meat on it. Puts one in her mouth. Then reaches for a bottle of pickled gherkins. Puts one into her mouth. Wipes her wet fingers on a shopping bag hanging there.

'As it happens I was calling Klepáč. I think he's got guests. There are lights everywhere in the house.'

Ludvík goes to the window. There's no doubt that his neighbour's house is unusually well-lit. Several black limousines can be seen through the trees. Silhouettes of men. Some people standing in front of lighted windows. It seems they are men too. As if that were not enough, in the garden the wind is picking up.

'I picked up her shopping in the government store. She paid for it in advance. Three Hungarian salamis. Anchovies. Four boxes of cheese. They really tuck in where cheese is concerned.' With the torch Anna lights up each item referred to in the pantry. 'The manager Tureček asked me to take it for her. Seeing that we were close by. Otherwise, a car would have to be sent here. Maybe she's already been to pick the stuff up. When we weren't here.'

By now Ludvík is in the hall.

He picks up the receiver. Holds it to his ear. No dialing tone. Shakes it. Clicks the cradle. Still not a peep to be heard from the receiver.

'You know what I think? That they were at the reception. In the spare drawing-room. Like the president always is. Tondl's wife told me that Klepáč is on track to become a minister. Is he bright enough for something like that?'

Anna returns to the pantry. Once again she has something in her hand that she's nibbling at.

Ludvík closes the door between the kitchen and the hall. Anna doesn't know that he's been trying the telephone.

'What did I tell you? Why are you closing... What have I just told you?'

'Don't shout.'

'You think I'm shouting? I can hardly hear myself speak. Please tell me what exactly I'm allowed to talk about at home. Go on. What can be talked about only in the kitchen, the bathroom, the loo? What can be mentioned as we go about our daily lives? You told me that in the kitchen, the bathroom and the loo we can speak about anything!'

Anna licks her fingers. And wipes them on the cloth.

'Is it a state secret that Comrade President has become a grandpa? Is that kept strictly under wraps? Is Ear allowed to hear this?'

Anna goes to the door to the hall. Leaves it wide open. Stands in the entrance hall looking into empty space.

And says out loud:

'Hey Ear! This is something for the record! Comrade President has become a grandpa! It's a boy! He's got all his bits in the right places! He's an eight-pounder! Unfortunately, the happy mother doesn't have enough milk.'

She closes the door. Turns to face Ludvík.

Ludvík is standing by the fridge with a bottle of vodka in his hands. He opens it. Extracts a glass from the cupboard in the half-light. It's the first his hand lights upon. The sound of sliding glass doors marks his clumsiness. It's a big glass. He pours himself a drink. A small one. Knocks the alcohol back with a gulp. Suddenly spits it out onto the linoleum.

'Jesus! What was in this glass? What did you put in it? Oh my God!'

Anna is already by the kitchen cupboard. She sniffs the glass. At the same time she holds a vodka glass up to Ludvík. One she's prepared for herself.

'I think I had acetate in that one', she says. 'I use it for my ankles. You know where all your things could be? Didn't I put them in that old wooden medicine chest? The one that had a lock? I fancy I stuffed them into something wooden!'

They go up the stairs. Ludvík is carrying the candlestick. With lighted candles. Anna has slung the fox fur over her bare arm. She has the unfinished bottle of vodka in her hand. 'It was the seventeenth of July ten years ago as well,' she says.

'It's the seventeenth of July again?'

'July the seventeenth comes every year,' says Anna. 'But you've never once remembered! Every year I have to be the one to remember! It's just too depressing! Too sad!'

'The 'phone was working last night, wasn't it...?' Ludvík remembers. He looks at Anna. 'Jindřich called, didn't he? To say he was going to be a bit late. That he was stopping for petrol...'

'I don't know about that,' she says. 'But it was working all right. The Čepická woman phoned me.'

She raises her free hand and unbuttons Ludvík's shirt collar.

She brushes against him with her hip. Reaches for the knot on his tie. Touches his neck. Ludvík remains entirely passive.

'That box is not in the cellar', he says. 'I didn't see the old medicine chest there.'

'It's here.' Suddenly Anna's voice becomes more conciliatory. 'Upstairs. In the spare room. Do you know what that Čepická woman wanted? She asked whether it was warm here during winter. In our own home. Markus from the government presidium has told her that our place will be vacant. That we're letting it go. What can you say about an idiot like that?'

Anna looks into empty space. Towards Ear.

'Joseph Markus!' she says. Out loud. 'Billeting official in the government presidium,' she says. 'Arsehole!'

'Do you have to repeat your performances on a daily basis?'

'Shame that you can't perform on a daily basis.'

Anna turns her back to him.

'Unzip me!'

They both come to a halt. Upstairs. There is a narrow corridor on this floor.

As there tends to be in small houses. And all kinds of doors. The staircase goes up still further: probably to an attic.

At last the zip has been unfastened. Without meaning to he produces a frisson.

'Hey... That tickles!'

Anna bursts out laughing.

'Comrades, we're off to bye-byes,' she says. 'Which means you can go to sleep too!'

He hails one of them. 'Rudolf!'. But the man slithers away to another cluster of people.

'Tonda!'

The one addressed is inspecting a tapestry and giving his undivided attention to chatting with his wife.

He places a hand on the shoulder of another: 'Hallo there, Bedřich!'

Bedřich swivels round sharply. He's clearly not pleased.

For a moment he stares in surprise. As if he has no idea who Ludvík is.

'You? Here....?'

'Where should I be? Why shouldn't I be here?'

'I thought... seeing that....' The rest of the sentence is swallowed up.

Ludvík wants to hear the rest of it. He wants it spelled out.

'Seeing that what...?' he says.

He doesn't take his eyes off the man.

'Seeing that....so many people are now somewhere else... I thought that you might also be... somewhere else. Gone away! Away from Prague...!'

'But we talked together on the phone this morning!'

Bedřich has completely forgotten that. Perhaps he has the impression that it took place ages ago or even that it never took place at all.

'I called about our report.'

'Aha! Of course! You're right! We did... speak ... this morning.'

The man laughs. But the laughter dies quickly.

'I have got so much on my plate... old fellow!' he says.

But all at once he takes a look around. It seems to Ludvík that he's watching to see who's looking at them.

Then he uses the same ploy as Ludvík:

'I must find Marie!' he says. 'You haven't seen Marie anywhere, have you? I'm looking for Marie...!'

He is standing by the window. He hears Anna calling from the bathroom:

'Another moment and we'll have to swim!'

Anna has the candlestick with her in the bathroom. Through the half-open door a dim light falls into the corridor.

'Are you getting out of your things?'

'Yes,' he says.

He can hear her plunging into the bath.

'Wow!' she calls. 'Just the thing!'

Ludvík is looking at the tarmac. And at the gate. And at a black limousine in front of the gate. He thinks he can make out people in the car.

The limousine is full. Pale oval faces looking as if they'd been pasted onto the car windows. He reckons all the men in the car are observing their house.

The top of his head is resting against the tiled wall of the Gents.

Inside the cubicle everything is very light. And decorated with nickel-plating. The main thing is that he's alone in there. He takes off his jacket. Hangs it over the door handle.

He can hear a man moving around on the far side of the door. Someone who spends perhaps half a minute trying to get in. For perhaps the sixth time he asks:

'Anyone there?'

Then he goes to the next cubicle.

Ludvík tries to take some deep breaths. To hold the contents of his stomach down. Holds a handkerchief at the ready. Suddenly he feels a wave of nausea and leans over the toilet bowl. At the same time he pulls the chain to flush it. The flow of water drowns out other sounds.

From somewhere he hears a voice:

'My God, someone's got a migraine in there.'

Two men emerge from the limousine. In coats. They approach the gate. Ludvík thinks they are shining a light onto the nameplate. One of them tries the handle.

'What are you doing...?' Anna calls out. 'Where are you?'

'I'll be right there.'

The flatfoots are in conference in front of the gate. Checking their watches.

18

They go down the stairs in a dignified manner. There are no longer any soldiers to provide them with a guard of honour. Just a few of the maintenance staff clearing away the pots of ivy.

Vagera comes tottering up to him. Breast heaving with medals.

He's already in his cups. 'Ludo,' he says. 'My bricklayer boy!'

He embraces Ludvík and winks. He can only move one of his eyes.

'I respect only those in trouble.' He gives a belch.

Fortunately, the car has just arrived.

A ton of beef leans out of the window. 'One hundred and seventeen!'

Why isn't it Jindřich?

'That's not my car', says Ludvík.

'It is your car, Comrade Deputy,' says a young officer from State Security. In a voice that brooks no dissent.

He opens the door. He looks Ludvík straight in the eyes.

'That's... not Jindřich,' says Anna. She is staggering a little. She seizes the driver by the nose. 'You... are not Jindra.'

Resigned to fate, Ludvík edges her forward: 'Just get in!'

'We live in Bulgaria Drive,' he says in the limousine.

'It's all right,' says Muscle, 'I know where I have to go.'

He feels terrible. He throws up, holding his briefcase in his hands. He has put the torch on the box of documents. He flushes.

Then he climbs onto the toilet seat. Lifts one hand holding a handkerchief while keeping the briefcase in the other hand and balancing against the wall. Dips the handkerchief into the cistern. Then gets down again. Shifts position so he can clean his trouser legs.

Breathing heavily. A loud sigh.

'Ludo!' He can hear Anna. On the other side of the door. Probably standing right up close to it. 'Are you unwell?'

'A bit,' he says.

In a chesty voice:

'Your stomach?'

'My stomach.'

'Shall I make you coffee?'

'No need...Did Jindřich say anything to you about not coming for us after the reception? Did he mention anything to you...?'

'He didn't say anything. Who brought us home? Who was it? He drove us all round Prague. Didn't you tell him where we lived?'

'Make me...a bit of coffee...'

He flushes the loo once more.

What did you eat there? You didn't eat those canapés with lobster again, did you?'

'No way...'

Anna sighs on the other side of the door.

'Every anniversary the same. Every one!... Whatever we do, we have a bad time.'

She goes off.

'Come on!' She is calling out to Ludvík again. From somewhere in the house. He hears her as she heads downstairs. 'Don't take too long about it!'

Ludvík is thinking about disposing with the handkerchief. It's dirty and it's wet. He cannot shove it into his pocket. He throws it down the loo. Kneels by the bowl. Opens his briefcase. Pulls out some papers, shines the torch on them, tears some to shreds. Tosses the shreds into the bowl.

Bent down and leaning forward, his face is caught in the light from the torch. Reproduced as a photograph, it could be of benefit to trainee psychiatrists. As a teaching aid.

He is standing on the edge of a small group surrounding a Comrade.

The Comrade knows that they have been waiting for him to speak. Meanwhile he searches for something to say.

'From boulders, comrades' he begins. 'We will raise the politics of the people from the finest blocks of stone. We must extend ourselves in every way. I know that it isn't easy...so that we can stand erect!' He pauses. People jostle one another to get into the salon.

Someone calls out: 'Silence! Silence!'

'The Comrade is speaking.'

'First and foremost, we are looking for...what is right,' he goes on. 'We are feeling our way. There are problems ahead. Great problems! We don't even know what they are. But what we must do is make up our minds one way or the other. We must. It can't be helped. I sometimes say to myself...Do I understand this? Do I understand that? I don't understand it! Very well. I can admit that. But what about the revolution? Is it waiting? Is it waiting for me to understand? We would not get the better of imperialism that way! So I make up my mind one way or another. And I can see that I have made the right decision. It didn't even hurt.'

Everyone starts to laugh. Even Ludvík is laughing.

'Only by deciding can we learn how to make decisions. Just as we only learn to swim... by swimming!'

Everyone applauds. Ludvík applauds too.

'I would go back to factory work like a shot. I would happily go for a drink on Sunday. To a football match. But that is not where we are heading, comrades! No rest for us, anymore. We are summoned to turn the world around! Mark my words! Not turn it upside down but turn it back the right way up, so that our heads are held high! For it is capitalism that has turned the world upside down!'

Applause. Someone shouts out 'Bravo!'

'How old is he?' asks someone in front of Ludvík. 'Sixty? Yes? Surely doesn't look it!'

'But don't go thinking... don't go thinking that everyone gets what I'm saying. We have comrade sirs of all kinds... Košaras come in many forms...'

Among the listeners there's a buzz of anticipation as the Comrade takes his time.

He looks deep in thought. Like someone who knows much more than he can say.

'Tondl!' He calls out the names. 'Klepáč, Šlesingr and associates!'

The buzz grows in volume. People chatter away. Full of anticipation.

'Košara...!' says the Comrade. In order to be heard above the buzz. 'For instance, Košara advises us not to shut down the old brickworks. And not to transfer people to where we need them. So that we avoid a lack of proportion... We say: No...! No, Mr Košara. A lack of proportion would arise if we allowed you and individuals like you to oppose the party line.'

Roars of applause. Ludvík joins in the cheering. He looks round. In case someone recognises him...

Later he's sitting in the luxurious cubicle. Porcelain bowl beneath a white lid. He sits on the lid and smokes a cigarette.

From outside he can hear the sound of footsteps, voices and flushing toilets. He is thinking things over. Then he remembers another detail: he reaches into his breast pocket, pulls out a wallet and feels with his fingers between its leather compartments until he finally fishes out a photograph.

He is on the photograph together with a smaller man who is bald. They are both standing by a cement mixer. At an exhibition of some kind.

Ludvík tears the photograph into several pieces. He gets up so that he can throw the fragments down the loo. Then he pulls the chain to flush them away.

He puts the cigarette back into his mouth. It has been in a wall-mounted ceramic ashtray.

He decamps from the cubicle only when it seems there's no one else in the cloakroom.

He goes to the entrance hall. Which is next to the grand department for taking a leak. And the washroom.

Ludvík goes into the washroom. Now he is really on his own.

Except for the elderly woman by the towels. She is standing by the wall near a basket of clean hand towels. She is so quiet she could be part of the furniture.

Ludvík washes his hands.

Above the sink there are liquid soap dispensers which are turned downwards for use.

Then the woman hands him a towel. He dries his hands.

He throws the used towel into the basket on the other side.

'Do you need scissors? Shall I bring you scissors? Here's your coffee. The water in the bath will already be cold.' Anna is again close by the door. His sanctuary.

'Look out of the window,' says Ludvík. Keeping his voice down. Now he's standing close to the door himself. 'That car – is it still by our gate?'

'What car?'

'An official one.'

'Official one?'

He hears Anna moving away. He flushes the loo.

He shines the torch onto the toilet bowl. The water level's rising. It's not flowing away. The bowl's full of shredded documents.

'But that's the car which parked there earlier!' says Anna. She is beginning to show a certain interest after all. 'They've moved away from the street light. They parked in a stupid place like complete idiots. Right under the light.'

'Are they in the car or standing in the street?'

'Why would they be standing in the street? Have you any idea why they'd do that when they've got things to do in the car?'

Anna can only explain things to herself in one way.

'What are you ripping apart in there...?'

'Where's the plunger?' he asks. 'Do you know where the plunger is? Wasn't there a plunger somewhere round here?'

'Oh my God, you haven't clogged up the loo, have you? Are you going to clean the toilet now?'

Ludvík flings open the door.

'Stop shouting like that!' he urges her. 'Walls have ears.'

Anna is ready for love in the sack. All she has on is a black chemise which stops at her hips. The fox fur is round her neck. Silver slippers on her feet.

She sees the detritus round the bowl. The papers all over the tiled flooring. The briefcase. Above all the change in Ludvík's features.

'So now you're sorting out your briefcase? Yes? Now?'

'Shhh!'

Ludvík is trying to listen.

'Is that someone knocking? Knocking on the gate?'

Anna begins to have her own suspicions.

Suddenly she looks as if she's paying attention.

'Who'd be knocking? Did you tell someone to drop by? Have you invited someone again?'

Ludvík walks the length of the corridor to the window. He positions himself so that no one can glimpse his profile from outside.

'Just remember that today I'm throwing everyone out,' says Anna. She goes up to Ludvík. 'Even if your Košara should come round.'

'Can't you just be quiet?'

'No, I can't. Tonight I won't have anyone coming here to spend the night prattling about brickworks. Not even the comrade minister. And me... like the idiot I am... making you coffee... and scrambling eggs... and listening to the latest ideas about cement mixers!'

The limousine Ludvík is watching has not changed its position in front of the gate.

He has not seen anyone on the pavement.

'How many of them are sitting inside?' whispers Ludvík. 'Can you see? Is it two or is it four?'

Anna tries to draw back the curtain.

'Leave the curtain alone,' he snaps at her.

'Two,' she says. 'I think there's two of them...Was it a foursome?' Her interest is aroused again.

'There were four of them,' he says. 'Perhaps the other two are in our garden.'

Ludvík drops this into the conversation.

But Anna cannot get the point.

'That must be it! Getting into our garden over the fence for some fun. You think so? They want to give me a ride! I bolted the gate, didn't I? Maybe all four are coming... Just like in the car... two in the front and two in the back.'

Only now does Ludvík notice Anna once again.

'Get dressed!' he says. 'Do me a favour, get dressed. At least stop gadding about here naked.'

Anna turns sharply to face him.

'Why should I get dressed? Tell me why, seeing that I've just got undressed. Does it now annoy you when I'm around without any clothes on? Since when? Can you tell me that? Maybe it wouldn't be a problem for you if someone else was here naked. Someone like the Konvičková woman...'

'Please!

'Up yours! You annoy me so much every time... Enough to make me...! I don't know why you must always annoy me so much. I'm not going to go down on my knees begging for it. I'm not in such dire straits, you know. Don't go thinking that. For all I care you can spend the rest of the night here doing somersaults!'

She turns away and heads for the bedroom in a huff.

'Don't get all wound up!' he says. 'It's my head...I don't know what's going on...'

Anna picks up the candlestick. She heads away from the corridor leaving him in the dark.

'I can tell you... exactly what's going on in your head. The government is going on in your head. Every other part of you is ripe for the disability pension.'

For Ludvík it is a liberation.

With a few isolated exceptions, women facing a crisis usually act to make the crisis worse.

He is taking action. He has gone to his study.

Ludvík's study is right next to the bedroom.

He shines the torch. Removes a drawer from the table and shoves the papers lying on the table into it as if it was the bin. Now the torch is between his teeth as he carries the drawer in his arms to the loo. Puts it down on the tiles.

He takes the torch in his hand once more and with the other opens the small window in the toilet. It opens onto a kind of cubbyhole. He feels around in it till at last he locates the rubber plunger.

He thinks he hears a noise. Like something banging inside the house. He listens out for a while but hears nothing more.

With his feet he shoves the drawer further into the small room to give himself space to close the door. He can hardly squeeze inside with the drawer there. But once the door behind his back has been bolted, he feels more secure even in this position.

He puts the torch back on the box of documents and leans forward.

Busies himself with the plunger for a while. Stirring things up in the bowl.

Until the water level really begins to drop.

Ludvík straightens himself up. He's breathing hard. No more strange noises to be heard at this point.

He puts away the plunger. Crouches down beside the toilet. Searches through his pockets for his lighter.

Then he sets fire to the first batch of official papers.

For a moment he holds a burning document between two fingers.

Then drops it into the bowl. Uses one burning document to light another. The recess is suddenly radiant.

Illuminating Ludvík's face in a crimson glow.

Several documents have been glued together and are so fat they will only burn at the edges. Ludvík is feeding the fire too impatiently. He pokes at half-burnt wads of paper with the handle of the plunger and even with his hands.

He burns his hands. Jerks away and licks a finger. Gets up. Swiftly pulls the chain.

To flush away the first batch.

Fumes rise from the red-hot bowl. The porcelain sizzles as it cools. Thick layers of smoke fill the little room. It is like being packed inside cotton wool.

A noisy procession is snaking its way through the rooms.

The singers are led by a heavily perspiring colonel.

'On both feet!'

The snake has to jump using both feet. And it's not allowed to tear itself apart.

'No falling out of line!'

Somebody asks Ludvík directly:

'What's your opinion...? About the Košara affair?'

'I don't know,' he hears himself say. 'I don't know, do you know?'

He is trying to look nothing but his normal self.

'But it's you who prepared the report on the brickworks for him. Didn't you?'

This unnerves him.

'Košara kept everything in his own hands,' he replies. 'He never let anyone near him. He did... All we did for him was... some groundwork.'

'On one foot!' the colonel calls out.

The singing snake starts hopping.

'Which foot?' they ask.

'The left one!'

The bystanders applaud. Somewhere the snake has come apart, with several women falling over. There's a burst of laughter.

Someone else buttonholes Ludvík:

'Košara understood all about it, wouldn't you say, Ludo? Put heart and soul into it? He was a builder at heart.'

The man is speaking quietly. Off the record.

Ludvík replies in his normal voice.

'Depends how you take it,' he says. 'Yes and no. He wasn't without flaws.'

'On your squatties!' the colonel calls out.

Now leading a squatting snake.

'On your squatties!' they call out. Several repeat the word.

Someone detaches himself from the chain and goes up to Ludvík.

'Comrade Deputy! Have you heard? About Košara?'

'Of course,' he says. 'Naturally I have.'

'But it's so...! What do you think? Do you understand what it's about? He had everything. That man had whatever he wanted. I will organise a party plenary at the ministry in the morning. We must arrive at an official position on the matter.'

'Naturally.'

'Backwards!' The colonel lifts his hand.

'About turn.'

It seems that at last everyone has fallen over.

Ludvík has got rid of the chap.

He notices a waiter with a tray of alcoholic drinks. Takes a glass. Drinks it in one. Grimaces in disgust. 'What's this you're handing out?'

'Pineapple liqueur. With vodka.'

'Who invented liquid manure like that, for Christ's sake?'

'The Comrade!' says the waiter.

Ludvík quickly turns away and hurries out. Taking the opposite side of the room to the waiter.

25

The wooden loo seat has caught fire. Ludvík's not good with his hands.

He's worn out and wound up.

When he suddenly wants to straighten himself up, he bangs his head on the box with the documents. It's quite a blow because he almost falls onto his knees, while one side of the box has become unhinged.

The torch has fallen onto the tiles. Fragments of glass fly everywhere.

Fortunately, the bulb isn't broken.

In any case there's light coming from the burning loo seat.

Ludvík pounds the burning varnish on the board with the plunger.

The singed rubber hisses.

He throws the plunger away. In the half-light. The torch is lying on the ground, shedding a dreary light like that of a cemetery candle.

Only a few things are left in the drawer.

He starts coughing and quickly turns round.

Someone is trying the door.

It's Anna.

'Ludo!' Her mouth must be at the key-hole. 'Ludvík...!'

She doesn't sound angry so much as anxious.

'What do you want?'

He doesn't move.

'Open up!'

'Why?'

'Please open up.'

Anna is whispering.

He opens the door.

She almost manages to cram herself inside.

With the dense smoke.

She has one foot in the drawer, almost breaking the bottom of it. She lifts her leg quickly while Ludvík picks up the drawer and puts it on the toilet seat.

Anna shuts the door behind her.

'There's some guy in the garden,' she says.

Ludvík realises that Anna has his binoculars in her hands.

'He's standing by the summerhouse. Always in the same... in that place. Why are you burning everything?'

'Didn't you put that report somewhere?' he says. 'The one I made notes in? That thick folder?

Anna cannot breathe properly. She can hardly speak.

Her eyes are fixed on Ludvík. And on the havoc around him. 'You've burned... our loo seat,' she notices. 'You mean the one about... about... the brickworks?

'Don't mention that word!' He hisses the warning at her. 'Everything said on the other side of this door is... on the record.'

'Yes, all right,' she says submissively. Her potato face is swollen.

'You put it on the table!'

'I know where I put it. I just don't know where it is now.'

'I never cleared any of your stuff from the table.'

'Take hold of this drawer! Hold the drawer...!'

He passes the drawer to Anna. Anna is standing right by the door with the drawer in her arms, while Ludvík kneels once again by the toilet bowl with some papers in his hands, using his lighter to set them on fire.

By now he has a definite routine based on folding each sheet to look like a paper tent and then releasing the burning documents into the toilet.

He feeds the flames with more folded papers. Every so often his face shows up, right next to Anna's bulky knees.

Anna is still dolled up in the same way.

'They haven't got a woman in that car!' says Anna. Now and again she glimpses Ludvík's head or his hands across from the drawer. 'There are two chaps there. I thought they might be going to call on Klepáč... maybe they can't find his place...? But all they do is sit there...! Ludo, why are you burning everything?' She is starting to cough.

She steps around his shoulders, holding the drawer, binoculars in one hand while with the other she opens a small window onto the ventilator.

'We'll suffocate in here, I can tell you.'

The breeze from the ventilator stirs up a few blackened remains.

What has not been burnt away glides around the loo past the maniacal features of Ludvík, who is trying to knock the half-burned pages down with his palm.

'Shut that!' he yells. 'Are you completely stupid?' He shakes a glowing document off his sleeve. He wants to straighten himself up so that he can shut the window himself. For the second time he hits his head. This time on the drawer, knocking it out of Anna's hand. The drawer falls onto the tiles with a crash. There's a crescendo of sound, because on top of her dropping the drawer he manages to kick it.

They are now stuck to one another. Back in the half-light, given that the fire from the burning papers has gone out.

'Quiet!' he says. 'For God's sake, be quiet!'

But everything is quiet now.

He tells Anna without moving, the words rushing out in one gasp as if they've been strung together:

'They've locked up Košara!'

At the same time, he pulls the chain and flushes the loo.

The water gurgles in the bowl.

'Tondl, Klepáč and Šlesingr as well,' he goes on. 'They've taken them in.' He's speaking quietly. He detaches himself from Anna and leans against the wall opposite. Even so they are huddled very close together.

'It happened straightaway as soon as they got there. They told them to go to...'

Once more he pulls the chain.

'...to this special lounge. That's where they copped it. What was that woman asking...?' Ludvík wants to use his hands to do up his shirt. All his buttons are undone. Anna had unfastened them on the stairs. He can't even do one up. In the end he manages to hold his shirt tight with his tie. 'What was that Čepická woman asking...?'

Anna breathes out:

'Whether our heating worked in the winter.'

Ludvík sits on the edge of the drawer standing up against the wall. Papers lie everywhere under his feet.

'That's it,' he protests.

Looking for a cigarette.

'Of course. Markus would know when a place has become vacant.'

26

They are still in the loo.

Ludvík is standing up, leaning his back against the door.

It's now Anna who sets to work. Using his lighter to set fire to documents.

While Ludvík has a cigarette.

Anna whispers:

'Should I burn the lot?'

'It doesn't matter anymore,' he says in a resigned voice. 'I couldn't care less now. If they're already... wait a moment. What was that?'

'Just the wind on the roof,' she says. 'Remember we've got a window open.'

Anna's voice is trembling. 'Those are your papers from the ministry. What on earth is in them?'

'Nothing. What should be in them?'

'If there's nothing in them... you've no need to burn them.'

'I've already told you to stop burning them. To hell with them.'

But Anna doesn't stop.

'But how can they... lock up a minister...?'

'From minstrels to ministers, they can lock up anyone they want,' he explains. He starts coughing again from the smoke. Then he speaks in a whisper: 'Do you know how many they put away in... that place? And how many of them... straight after being locked up with no time wasted on procedures... ended up like that?'

He makes a gesture whose meaning is clear.

It's made even clearer by the fact that he obviously doesn't want to shock Anna. Or scare her. He is just stating how things are. As if she wasn't even there.

'Where?' she asks. 'Where?'

'Where do you think?'

'Russia?'

He flushes the loo once again.

'Maybe they will only want... information.' He's now talking to himself. He's looking at the ceiling. 'Seeing I was his first deputy.'

She turns round.

'You were...?' she begins.

She stares at Ludvík for a moment.

'You're no longer deputy?'

Only now does he take in Anna's presence.

'I am deputy. Why shouldn't I be? I suppose I still am. Who's who and who isn't... who knows any longer.'

27

'Couldn't we do the burning in the laundry room? Under the boiler?' she asks.

'We can be seen from the garden there.'

Ludvík has been thinking about this.

They are still in the loo.

Anna can't get the lighter to work.

'It doesn't ignite anymore,' she says.

'Fetch the candle,' he says. 'You left the candles somewhere, didn't you?'

Anna is kneeling on the tiles. She lifts her head.

'Why me? You're the one who's by the door.'

'Give me that.' He holds out his hand to take the lighter. He turns it over in his fist so that the flint and the wick face downwards. Holds it like that for a while. Flicks the lighter. The flame catches.

He passes the lighter to Anna. So that she can burn the last documents.

'We should have stayed in Olomouc,' says Anna. She blows her nose. With the back of her arm she wipes her wet nose. Whenever the fox fur slips down onto her lap while she's bending forward, she returns it to her back with a flick of her torso. 'We should never have moved to Prague! What were we missing there? We had a car just like we do here. We had somewhere to live like here. But with you it was always... Košara needs me, Košara this, Košara that. He doesn't have decent people around him! Who knows where Košara will go next, perhaps they'll finally make me the minister...'

'Go on, why don't you shout it from the rooftops?'

'I'm not saying anything that can't be heard. I can speak to anyone face to face. I don't have any secrets!'

'And I do? I do have secrets?'

'How would I know.'

'You were in Prague before I was. I wasn't even here. Who was the first to come rushing here?'

'Who sent the car to get me? Who was that? Košara! And who put ideas into his head? About showing me the villa....? Knowing that I didn't want to go to Prague...'

Ludvík reaches swiftly across Anna's shoulders to the door of the toilet.

'What is it you're burning here...? What's this?'

He tries to stop a piece of paper burning, presses it against the wall and beats it with the palm of his hand.

Anna lifts herself up.

She turns to Ludvík. She looks at what he's holding in his hand.

'It's Luděk's school report'.

'What would Luděk's school report be doing in my drawer?'

'I put it there for you. To stop you telling me that you're not kept informed.'

'Why are you always meddling with my things? Going through my drawers, my pockets, my briefcase. Do I bother myself with your things?'

'No,' she says. She gets even closer to him as she speaks. 'You've never bothered with anyone. You've only ever cared about yourself.' She takes the school report out of his hand.

The bottom part of it is singed.

'Where are we going to sign it now?' she says. 'It has to be signed and returned.'

'For God's sake!' He heaves a deep sigh.

He throws the cigarette butt down the loo.

The paper isn't burning any more. There's just a hissing sound. The loo is in semi-darkness with only a weak bulb to provide light.

'Don't talk to me like that,' she says, taking offence. She wants to pick up the empty drawer but manages to make it crash onto the floor, next to the toilet bowl.

The sound can be heard all over the house.

'Have you gone mad?'

Ludvík is listening out.

'Mad at you.' She is speaking out loud.

She is sensitive about certain things, no doubting that.

'If you took more care of these things and less of... I don't know what... you wouldn't need to get into a panic now.'

'I...? You think I'm panicking?

He is whispering.

'No,' she says, still raising her voice. 'I'm the only one who's panicking. The thing is that I tell you when I panic, whereas you say nothing even though you're shitting yourself. That's the difference between us.'

Anna pushes him to one side and reaches for the door handle.

'Where are you going?'

'To get some clothes on. I'm not going to prance around as if I was in Hawaii. Is the lavatory going to be your home until morning...?'

Anna is opening the window in the corridor. Ludvík is standing in the loo holding the drawer in one hand and the torch with its faint glimmer in the other.

The open door to the bedroom allows the light from the candle there to cast a red glow into the corridor.

'Don't open that!'

'We don't want it to be like a chimney here. That would get them thinking, it surely would. Thinking that we were...'

'Anna!'

Looking terrified he alerts her to Ear.

'Oh,' she says in answer to his terror. 'I know.'

'Look,' she hisses. 'Ludo!' She summons Ludvík to the window.

'Close the door to the bedroom! Switch off the torch!'

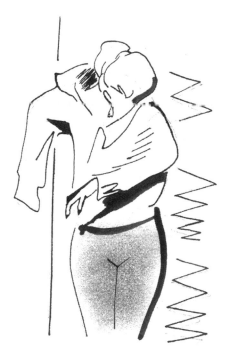

He goes up to her. It's pitch black now.

'He's not standing by the summerhouse anymore,' whispers Anna. 'Can you see him? Do you see him right there? Standing by that tree...'

Ludvík can already see the man.

He's wearing a light raincoat. Standing by a freshly trimmed ornamental tree. He appears to be looking at the house.

'You keep a pistol in your table,' says Anna. 'What if they're just common thieves....?'

At that moment a loud bang is heard inside the house. They both freeze.

Without thinking Anna grabs Ludvík's hand.

But Ludvík drags her into the bathroom. And shuts the door.

'Just answer their questions!' There's an urgency in his voice. Surprisingly enough, he's acting now with a cold calm. As if the men were already there.

'Only reply to what they ask you...! Don't tell them that Košara is our Luděk's godfather. They'd see it as...who knows what they'd see in it!'

Anna reaches a hand into the bath and pulls out the plug.

It's a nervous reaction on her part. Then she stands up. She thinks for a while. With her mouth open. Opens the door.

'Did you shut the window in the laundry-room?' she asks.

'Yes....'

'You didn't shut it! You didn't shut the door of the laundry-room either. It was the draught that caused the banging. When I opened the window here.'

Ludvík puts the torch down on the table.

The tiny bulb throws a beam of light onto the ceiling.

He returns the drawer to its place. Likewise the brief-case, which goes next to the table. In his agitated frame of mind, he can't get the drawer in properly.

At first, he tries to be delicate. Fixes his mind on the task in hand. But it doesn't take long for him to lose patience and start cramming the drawer into the table.

As he struggles to shove the drawer in it gets jammed. He tries forcing it further in and finds that he can neither get it right in nor pull it out.

He gives up on the drawer.

'Get changed!' he hears Anna saying. From the bedroom. Where she's changing. The bedroom is connected to Ludvík's study by an internal door which is half-open.

Anna throws him a hanger through the door into the study. It lands on the carpet.

'Make sure you hang your glad rags,' she says.

Ludvík is sitting on a chair. He takes out a cigarette. Lights it.

'I just don't know what he cooked up for that report in the end! He did the final version... himself!' He speaks so that Anna is able to hear him. 'You know what he was like! When someone gave him a piece of advice. I told you how we had so many rows...!'

'But Košara listened to you,' says Anna. Naively. 'He liked you.'

'When I was his yes man... You should have seen what it was like when I tried to say 'No'. Did I tell you how we fought one another in committee? The way he looked at me then?'

'No! You didn't tell me.'

Anna appears for a moment in the doorway. She already has her bra on. And tracksuit bottoms. With white stripes down the sides. She is dragging a matching top over her head.

'And as for Klepáč... and Tondl... as for, whatsisname, Šlesingr, I didn't even know them...'

Ludvík is saying all this out loud. He is speaking only to Anna, but it is as if he is speaking for the benefit of Ear.

Anna trips over the hanger lying on the carpet. Instead of picking it up she kicks it out of the way.

'But you did know Šlesingr... well!' she says. 'Weren't you at the party's training academy together...? You even said that he... had his head in the right place!'

Ludvík gets up suddenly and is standing right next to Anna.

'Are you out of your mind?' he hisses. Quietly. 'How can you bellow out something like...'

Anna has no idea what she's done.

'You're speaking louder than I am,' she says to defend herself.

Ludvík taps the side of his head with a finger. Peevishly.

'The point is that I know what I'm saying,' he sighs. 'Set that alarm clock of yours.'

Hurriedly they sort through the pile of odds and ends. Re-arranging the wicker furniture as they go. The porcelain inside the cardboard boxes clinks as they rummage around.

They are in a place which serves as a storage-room. They have the candlestick and the torch at hand.

'There was that large box which Aunt Božena had in her workshop', says Anna. 'She kept the medicine chest inside it.'

Ludvík shines the torch around as if he's suddenly thought of something.

By the wall there are three sewing machines! Industrial-grade Singer sewing-machines. They are joined by a few tailors' dummies! There are also boxes with special irons used by tailors.

'My God! So your aunt never managed to take them away?' he protests.

'Is her junk going to stay clogging up the place forever? How many times have I said that she should get it out of here? How many times have I said to you...?'

'Where? Take it where? They took her house, they took her flat, they took her cottage. Should she keep it in the one room they left her with?'

'Couldn't it go to a scrapyard?'

'Good idea! Carry off new Singer sewing machines to the scrap heap. They're brand-new ones! You yourself told her not to sell them. That the currency would be worthless...'

'Shhh!'

Anna is speaking in a whisper now:

'This is somewhere we can speak, isn't it? Ear can't get to us here. We told them we were going to use this space for the children. The Klepáč woman said that they don't eavesdrop on the children's room. When they have visitors, they make sure they're sitting in the children's....'

'Yes, and just think where it is they're sitting now,' he says. He goes out of the room feeling vexed. As he leaves, he gestures for Anna to follow him.

They go to the bathroom.

Leaving the torch and the candlestick in the storeroom. Ludvík closes the door.

They stand in the bathroom where it is pitch black.

This is how they have more intimate conversations.

'What are we going to tell them...?' he says. He speaks as if he's talking to himself rather than to Anna.

'Where did we get these machines from? I should have thrown the barmy old bat out. I should have taken her by the scruff of the neck and shown her the door.'

'You said yourself that she could store her carpets in our place.'

'Carpets! Carpets are no problem! We just unroll them and it's as if they're our carpets!'

Ludvík gets the water running. Slaps cold water onto his face. Sighs.

Reaches for a towel to get himself dry. While he does so, he becomes aware of what he's using to dry himself. 'What's this? What rags have you got hanging here?'

Anna takes it away from him.

'That's my slip.'

'Do you think they're going to come creeping into the house...? Crawling from one door to another?'

'Going through the kitchen dresser mug by mug!'

Something has occurred to him.

'The Women's Committee!' he says. 'You're still on the Women's Committee, aren't you?'

'Yes...What of it?'

Ludvík steps right up to Anna.

'Tell them your aunt was self-employed. Don't hide anything from them. Tell them exactly what she was like. How

(72)

penny pinching she was. That way they'll know you feel the right way about her.'

Ludvík is speaking anxiously as if they have already moved to the other side of the bathroom door.

'Say that she wanted to flog the machines... but that I told you... No, don't mention my name in connection with the machines!' He is trying hard to think.

'Say that I never cared about such things. That I was always at the ministry... and that you told your aunt not to sell them. She should give them to you instead. And then you put them at the disposal of the... women's committee! Don't you have sewing clubs there?'

This all seems like a very good idea to Ludvík.

'Where did I leave my cigarette? I put it down somewhere...'

He runs out of the door.

Anna doesn't move.

Ludvík comes back. With the cigarette.

'Can you remember what we've said? Have you got it?'

'No,' she replies, taking offence. 'I'd need it written down. Otherwise, I might let the cat out of the bag by saying Auntie gave us a hundred and fifty thousand crowns.'

He quickly sends water gushing into the bath.

Hoping to drown her out.

Despite the darkness his face looks completely green.

'Why should they believe this story about the machines?' Anna is looking at Ludvík. 'Even the cops can't be that stupid.'

She hangs the slip over the door handle.

He removes it and reaches out a hand to hang it on a peg. Full of agitation, he puts out his cigarette under the tap.

And now flushes the stub away.

'They might believe it because it's not true. It's the stuff that's true they won't be able to believe.'

'When we were standing in the cloakroom... you remember? And off went comrade... you were standing there with Blková. Vágnerová as well... the Comrade went straight up to you... he said something to you, didn't he? What did he say to you?...'

They are back once again with all the odds and ends.

Like a miner straining at the coal face, Ludvík is shovelling junk out of the way.

Anna is standing at the window looking out into the garden.

'The Comrade knows you...We were in the official residence of the president. At one of those party functions they have around Christmas. We went through the park after that and you lost your shoes in a snowdrift. Yes, the Comrade remembers who you are all right...'

There is an urgency in his voice as he speaks to Anna.

She turns to face him.

'You're right, he does', she realises. 'It was when there were all those roses. All the old women made a beeline for them! They were down to the last vase. The Comrade didn't know which one to give them to... And he said... But I don't know exactly what he said. I can't recall it. He said something to me...'

'Can't you remember what he said?'

Beads of sweat have appeared on Ludvík's forehead. The drops trickle down around his eyes. And onto his face. But he remains unaware of this.

'Try and remember what he said! Try!'

But Anna has gone back to looking at the garden.

'There's another one standing there,' she whispers. 'Another snooper right there.'

Ludvík draws himself up and blows out the candles.

He can't turn off the torch, so he stuffs it into his pocket while it's switched on.

'Where...? Where...?'

He gasps out the words as if his jaw isn't working.

'Can't you see him? By the bench...? Where those trees are.'

Ludvík has already spotted him.

The man is almost camouflaged by the bushes. He's facing the house. Like as not right opposite the window which they have just plunged into darkness. Then the man steps back a little. As if he can feel himself being observed.

The Comrade is smiling like a benign deity.

In his hands he's holding the vase of roses.

He knows that everyone is looking at him. He always wears an expression that says he has no inkling of being the centre of attention.

'Now which female comrade has her name day today?' He lifts up the vase. 'Which young woman...? Girls!'

All the women are laughing.

'It's me' says Anna. She raises her hand. She speaks as if she's in the classroom.

'I have a special day today.'

She's blushing.

One of the women objects:

'How can it be Anna's name day today? Since when has there been an Anna at this point in the calendar?'

'It's my anniversary!' explains Anna. She looks at the Comrade. 'I was married ten years ago today.'

'Your identity card....' says the Comrade. 'We have to take our female comrades at their word... But we must verify what they say.'

'My ring!' says Anna. She slips the ring off her finger.

'It has the date on it.'

The Comrade does indeed take the ring. He has put down the vase in order to do so.

He puts on his glasses. But he can see nothing through them. He takes them off.

'How come... I've got a certain woman's glasses in my pocket?' he asks.

More general merriment.

'Where can they be...? My glasses...?'

At last he manages to put on his own glasses.

And reads the date on the ring.

'The 17th of the 7th,' he says. 'And raises lascivious eyes towards Anna. 'Comrade Anna's telling the truth.'

At this moment someone whispers in his ear.

The Comrade keeps looking at Anna. He starts to look more serious.

But then he says: 'Promises must be kept!'

He hands the flowers and the antique vase over to Anna.

He gives her back the ring.

'So may you have many... offspring... comrade. To replenish our ranks!'

He turns round. Quickly. Too quickly. And goes out.

Anna is holding the magnificent vase in her hands. And the roses. She is alone. All of a sudden no one is interested in her.

She takes a few uncertain steps out to the cloakroom.

And then an elegant man slides up to her.

'I will wrap the roses in paper for you,' he says to Anna.

'I am afraid to say that the vase must remain here! The Comrade was not well-informed about such... minor details.'

33

'You're sure he mentioned you by name? Called you "Anna"...?'

'I think so.'

'He did or he didn't?'

'I'm not sure. I don't know any more. I'd had a bit to drink...'

'A bit! Did he seem to know who you were...? Did he appear to recognise you?'

'If he knows me, then he recognised me, don't you think? Or maybe he's losing his marbles.'

'Pay attention, for God's sake! If he said "Anna", if he was all smiles and welcoming... it must have meant something! Meant something politically. He knows you're my wife and if I was ever... if I was in hot water of some kind, then he'd know... and he wouldn't call you "Anna" then!'

'He did call me "Anna"!'

She nudges Ludvík. 'There's a third one!' she says. 'Number Three is over there!'

The snooper opens a small gate concealed in the fence. Then he edges his way towards the man they'd seen earlier.

'They were in the Klepáč place!' Anna confirms. 'Now he's closing the gate! Can you see him? I mean the little old connecting gate behind the compost heap... we'd forgotten all about it!'

She feels relieved.

'But that gate... wasn't it wired shut?'

'It's not wired shut!' she says. 'The Klepáč woman and I removed the wire. So that we didn't have to traipse along half the street! When it was only a few steps across the garden to call on each other. We took turns, each of us cooking only one day in two. Do you think they'll move her out and stick her into a flat? Now that he's been... put away?'

Ludvík turns round. Spends a while staring at Anna as if his cervical vertebrae have been immobilised.

'Why didn't you ever tell me about this gate?'

'When was the last time you showed any interest in what I had to say to you? The Klepáč woman really was a good cook. If her stuff had tasted like horse manure, I wouldn't have bothered with her. Don't you understand that? Do you think I'm not right in the head?'

Ludvík taps his temple.

The men are now clearly visible.

Crossing the grass. Going up to the fence.

One of them bends down in the vegetable plot.

'He's picking our radishes!' says Anna. 'Can't they walk on the paths?'

They are going through the gate. Onto the pavement. Into the limousine. The last one out locks up.

'Where did they get a key from?'

'Getting keys is not a problem for them,' says Ludvík.

Once again his throat is struggling to release words.

The men are already sitting in the car.

The limousine picks up speed without a sound. No engine involved. As if the brakes released themselves.

34

And then the lights come on. All at once.

In the sudden glare from electric bulbs they both look green. As if they've just come flowing in from a fish tank.

Anna has limp hair and a tired face.

Ludvík steps back from the window. Starts switching off lights hurriedly. Wherever he switched lights on beforehand. Corridor. Bedroom. Bathroom. Study. Bathed in the light, Anna's sloppiness loses its romantic appeal. Several pairs of shoes are scattered over the floor. She probably tried them all on before they went to the reception.

Ludvík runs down into the hall. Switches out the light in the kitchen. Then he stands by the kitchen window. The neighbour's villa is dark now. In the garden the wind seems to have strengthened during the night.

He turns round. Goes back to the hall. Lifts up the receiver. Hears the dialing tone coming through clearly. Spends a moment in thought. As if there was some number he wanted to dial. Then puts the 'phone down again.

Anna appears on the staircase at this moment. Dragging a white crate.

'I ask you, it was right at the top all along! How come you couldn't find it? You must have been looking right at the wretched thing.'

She dumps the crate halfway down the stairs.

'You know who it maybe was....?' says Anna. She is bearing Ear's presence in mind. 'Rag-and-bone men. They're always passing up and down the street. Last time we found them in the garage when it was raining. We didn't even know about them being there.'

'Oh no!' says Ludvík, sounding annoyed. 'It wasn't this I was looking for. He rummages in the crate. Finds textbooks and notebooks. ARITHMETIC. SURVEYING. BUILDING MATERIALS. 'This is stuff from technical college. You could have chucked it out ages ago.'

'Don't you think it could have been rag-and-bone men?'

'No', he says. Quietly. 'Since when have they been driven around in official cars? They'd go from street to street on foot. They wouldn't hang around in gardens.'

'Why not? Who knows whether they all stick to their official duties! Do you think they're all like you? Only interested in work?'

Ludvík is kneeling down by the crate.

'I've never been able to find anything in this place! Never!'

'Me neither,' she says. 'But I'm not one to make such a song and dance about it.'

Anna heads downstairs to the kitchen. Heads for the fridge. Opens it.

The light comes on inside the fridge.

She reaches in. Grabs a schnitzel.

Holds it in her fingers. Takes one bite after another.

Bangs the fridge door shut.

Even she can't resist stopping by the window. She looks across at the neighbour's house. Goes back to the hall. And up the staircase.

'Isn't it just a wild rumour? About Klepáč and Košara? Who told you all this? Could we be making fools of ourselves? Maybe the comrades and the comradesses were having rumpy pumpy together. Who knows whether the scoundrels weren't just invited over for... a party?'

'Do you have to go on all the time? Couldn't you just for a moment stop banging on?'

By now Ludvík has pulled everything out of the box. Notebooks, textbooks and materials for drawing lie scattered around him. On the stairs.

Anna stops next to him.

When she stands next to him, he has his head at the same level as Anna's broad thighs. But he carries on as if Anna's not there. It doesn't take Anna long to get the point. She purses her lips.

'You needn't bother changing out of your formal gear at this point,' she says, assuming an air of indifference.

'The binmen come tomorrow. I'll let them have the stuff as a present. They can still make use of it at work for a while.'

She stops wasting her time on Ludvík. Feeling offended, she takes the thighs away.

It's not long before he catches up with her.

'Didn't we put my things in one of those boxes in the garage?'

Anna is armed with bucket and rag inside the loo. The lid is up. She's washing the seat.

'Don't speak to me,' she says.

'Must you be cleaning the throne room right now?'

'Before I sit on something, I like to know what I'm sitting on!' she says. 'There's nothing in the garage. Nothing but things from the pub.' She's still worried by the seat. She tries to peel off or smooth down hardened blisters of burnt paint. Using the handle of the plunger. 'Before I sit down on this I'll need armour plating on my bum. Could you bring me sandpaper from the kitchen...?'

'Now I know where those things are,' Ludvík remembers. 'In my military suitcase. That's where we put the things. Now where is that suitcase...?'

'I wouldn't know. It wasn't me who did military service. Maybe it's in the cellar.'

'I didn't see it in the cellar.'

'Where else would it be?'

Anna thinks about this while she's kneeling on the tiled floor.

She is by the bowl. Ludvík is standing right above her. But before either of them can put a suggestion into words, the bell rings. Several times. At regular intervals.

'Telephone!' she says. She thinks it's the 'phone ringing.

'That's not the telephone,' he says.

Anna gets to her feet. Looks straight at Ludvík.

Both are now standing and facing one another.

Meanwhile the ringing goes on.

'It's coming from the gate, isn't it?'

'Yes,' says Ludvík. He looks as if there isn't a single red blood cell left in his body. 'From the gate.'

She wants to put the light out. In the corridor.

'Don't put the light out!'

The bell is now ringing continuously.

'That would... they'd see it at once!'

He keeps away from the window. Goes to the bedroom.

It's dark in the bedroom.

Anna follows hard on the heels of Ludvík.

'Shut the door! Shut it... so that... nothing lets the light in here.'

Now she too can see in front of the gate.

Two cars are standing in front of the gate.

There are several men on the pavement...

They are back inside the loo.

'If they haven't noticed... the suitcase!' Ludvík's voice falters. 'If by some chance they haven't noticed... then... get rid of it somewhere. Or burn it... but not here. They'll pick through everything here.'

She kisses Ludvík forcefully.

'Ludo,' she sobs, unable to hold back tears. 'Ludo!'

'Stop wailing like that. Please stop it.'

She stops. Tries to stop. 'What... what will become of us? Of little Ludi? Of me?'

'I'm going to open the door to them,' he says. 'Don't be afraid. Nothing's going to... happen to you.' He stumbles over his words.

'Take the deposit books for the bank and your... gold powder compact! Your rings too! And find somewhere to put all those things. They will crawl through everything you have. Make sure we have some money left.'

'Ludo, you haven't done anything... you really wouldn't have done anything!' She wipes her nose. 'I know you only too well... you've always been too scared to get mixed up in anything...'

'Did you understand me about what you have to do?'

'Where do I have to put...?'

He has sudden inspiration. 'With the boy's stuff,' he exclaims while keeping his voice down.

'Stuff it into his satchel! Among his school things. There's a chance that if it's there... there's a chance... they might not...'

He's frantically changing his clothes.

The bell keeps ringing.

He leaves the clothes which he's taken off lying on the floor. Steps on them as he pulls on a vest.

'My long johns!' he says. 'Where are they?'

'Long johns?'

'Come on!'

He pulls the long johns over his underpants.

'Brown suit,' he says. 'Brown... woollen... suit.'

He stuffs a foot into a trouser leg. In his exasperation he several times manages to step over rather than into the trouser leg.

'Mummy! Mummy...!' comes a young lad's voice from somewhere in the house. 'Someone's ringing.'

'I know,' Anna shouts out. 'Go back to sleep!'

'My sweater!'

'Wouldn't you rather have a shirt?'

'I said "sweater".'

'Won't you be too warm in that?'

'Better too warm than too cold.'

He puts a jacket on over the sweater. But he's still in his socks.

He dives into the wardrobe.

'Where are my shoes... the sturdy low ones with the metal toe?'

Anna hands the shoes to him.

He forces his heels inside them.

'Go to the window,' Ludvík says. 'Shout from the window that I'm coming... if only they'd stop ringing, for Heaven's sake!'

Anna opens the window.

Ludvík is already on the staircase. He catches sight of the crate. Which he'd completely forgotten about. He kneels down. Almost falls down. Hurriedly flings notebooks and textbooks into it. Comes back with the crate.

He hears Anna calling out to the men at the gate.

'He's coming! He'll be right with you!'

He gets the impression that the men greet Anna.

At last the bell falls silent.

He tosses the crate in among a pile of junk. In the spare room.

He goes into his study and fetches several packets of cigarettes from the table.

'The lighter!' he says. 'In my trousers!'

Anna looks in the trousers he's just taken off.

At last she finds the lighter. And throws the trousers back onto the floor.

'I haven't done anything!' says Ludvík. Out loud. 'Not a thing,' he says. 'On my word of honour.'

He is speaking to Anna. And to Ear. There's a tremor in his chin. He's not a hero. His fear is plain to see. Swiftly he turns round.

Goes into the corridor. Calmly, it would seem. Goes down the stairs. For a moment he finds himself unable to unlock the door. He's so tense he double locks it instead. He shakes the handle. At last he manages to unlock.

He feels the blustery air in the garden on his face.

There are three low steps leading down from the door to the concrete pathway. He doesn't see them, forgets about them in his anxiety and stumbles.

The cars by the gate have their headlights on full.

The area is flooded in light. Ludvík thinks that there's someone's head above the fence. He hears someone's voice saying clearly:

"He's coming! He'll be right here!'

Suddenly he feels his strength draining away together with his will to go on. To go up to the gate. He has to stop.

He tries lighting a cigarette. His lighter's on its last legs.

It fails to ignite. What he really wants to do is look around. His eyes roam as he tries to think some other options into existence.

'Is he coming...?' he hears from the gate. 'Is he on his way?'

'He's just standing there gawping.'

'Call him. That should stop him gawping.'

'Wait a moment.'

The dark outline of two heads appears above the fence.

But Ludvík is concentrating on the summerhouse.

There's a man standing there. Half-hidden by shrubbery. White raincoat, white face.

At this very moment Anna runs out of the house.

Probably she hasn't done anything that he asked her to do.

She is bringing Ludvík his briefcase.

'Take your briefcase,' she says, sounding out of breath. 'I've packed some stuff for you in there!'

She seizes Ludvík by the hand.

'She's coming too,' says the voice at the gate. 'He's coming out with his woman.'

That wasn't a comment meant for his ears. He hears it all the same.

All of a sudden, he doesn't want her to be there with him.

'Don't go with me...!' he says. Very gently.

'This is best done... on my own.'

He hadn't spoken to her so graciously all evening...in fact not for donkey's years.

'I put in your pyjamas...'

Ludvík is already going. Anna is at his side, holding on to him all the time. '...three shirts... and socks... and handkerchiefs!'

'Go back,' he whispers. 'Please...'

He turns to Anna. 'Go... to my desk,' he says. 'I have some little capsules with lighter fuel there... Bring me two or three for my lighter. But you must be quick... before... before...'

'Yes,' she says. 'Of course.'

She is surprisingly sober now.

'Hello there!' a chap calls out from the gate.

'Yes, I can hear you,' Ludvík calls back.

'In the bottom drawer,' he says. To Anna this time.

'Be right with you,' he calls out. 'I'm right here.'

'She's going back in', he overhears. 'She's going away.'

Ludvík's keys jangle as he looks for the one to the gate.

'I'll be... right... with you' he says in a tone of willing cooperation.

One man jumps down from the low wall. A second man keeps his head at all times above the gate.

Which at this moment means above Ludvík.

Ludvík is aware of this. He acts as if he isn't.

'Which one of these keys is it...?' Ludvík says to himself out loud. It's not conscious prevarication. He wants to indicate to them that he's not trying to stretch things out deliberately. He just can't remember. His fingers are numb. But he's trying.

'The nickel one!' says the head. From above the gate. 'The long nickel one'. Ludvík looks up.

The head grins back at him.

And at that very moment, before he's able to insert the key which he's at last got hold of, there's the rattle of a key already inside the lock. A key that has been inserted from the other side of the gate.

The gate opens.

With a swing...!

Opens towards Ludvík. Towards the interior.

He can barely move out of the way.

He finds himself face to face with other faces.

Those of six men. Perhaps seven.

In his agitation he cannot work out how many of them have come for him.

40

'Your bell jams! I only wanted to give a light ring and... it went haywire! What a bitch! Does it always freak out like that?'

'No,' says Ludvík, 'At least I don't know... it's never yet... but of course... it's possible...'

'No doubt about it', says Orangutan. 'I had to give it a poke... nudge it with my knife.'

Ludvík notices a dagger in the man's hand. Now the man releases an invisible catch. The gleaming blade is retracted into the solid knife-handle. The mechanism does its work with a sharp click!

'We could have unlocked the gate ourselves,' says a second man. With a wide grin. 'With these keys here,' he says. He takes them out of the lock.

'This little latchkey is for the front door? Am I right?'

'These would be your keys, wouldn't they?' says a third man. He fixes Ludvík with a look of curiosity. His face seems to have more width than height. He appears to be missing a forehead too.

'That's right,' says Ludvík. 'I think they are... our keys. My wife had them in her cape and she must have...lost them somewhere.'

'They're your keys, no doubt about it.'

Colossus is standing directly in front of Ludvík. He's breathing right into his face.

'Take hold of them. Touch them. You're quite sure...'

'Yes... otherwise... they wouldn't fit... the gate!'

'Say no more! You left them there. In the cloakroom! We said that we had to bring them to you here... at once... fetch them... so you wouldn't worry that someone had pinched them. It was Standa who said we should do it... but...'

'...he hasn't survived the journey,' explains another man. 'He's lost it a bit.'

It's only now that Ludvík pulls himself together.

Manages to take it all in. And take a good look at the men.

He notices they don't look like officials armed with arrest warrants. They look more as if they've just come from a brewery.

They stand to one side. Stanislav is at the back. Sitting on the sidewalk. Away with the fairies. Head leaning on the low brick wall. Graze on his forehead. He's rolled both trouser legs up above his knees. Or they've rolled themselves up. Hairy calves with unfastened garters.

'Rudy...! Joey...!. Lift him up, you blockheads! Before the cold blows up his arse.'

They lift him up.

Stanislav raises his head.

'Are we getting wasted?' he shouts out. 'Lads, are we getting wasted... who's got the fuel can...?'

'You threw the can at that clown in Wenceslas Square, you nincompoop! The traffic police will get their knickers in a twist about that, all right!'

'Let's get wasted!' Stanislav doesn't want to listen to anything. 'I'm firing on all cylinders!'

'Just look at you, totally out of it! Attention!' Orangutan shouts back. At Stanislav. Evidently Orangutan is the authority figure among these men. 'Stand to attention. Let him go! Don't hold him up! He's got legs of his own!'

'Lads! Don't let gravity get to me!'

'Let him go, I said! Open those peepers. How can you get wasted like that? When you're about to catch up with your best mate...'

'Ludo!' says Stanislav. Now he's spotted Ludvík and is clearly delighted.

'Friends, this is... my best fff...riend! Ludo! The minister!' he says. 'The minister... meet your blockheads... Here they are, Ludo! My best classmates! I take that back.' He corrects himself. Mumbling as he goes. Takes a while to think. Tries as hard as he can. 'My best... workmates!'

'Koštálek!' bellows their commanding officer. 'Lieutenant Koštálek.'

'No giving names! No giving names!' The admonition comes from the bulky leader of the herd. 'No real names. Only aliases.'

'Standa!' Colossus corrects himself.

'Yes,' says Stanislav. 'Pseudonyms! Every organ of state has... pseudonyms.' He's struggling to keep his balance.

'These are... Ludo... these are men of letters... these are the brothers Prim...'

He collapses onto the ground.

'Sorry about that,' says another man. Who until this point has been lurking at the back. He is the only one who doesn't look as if he escaped from a labour camp an hour earlier.

'The man's a bit under the weather.'

41

'My old mate!' he hears from behind his back.

He turns round and sees Broken Nose.

'Don't you recognise me? What sort of fellow doesn't know his old pal when he sees him? We were always chasing tail during our military service. You were the one climbing through the window of that school in Opava and I was the one slipping that hot girl a length at the train station.'

'Ah!.. Ah-ha!.. Oh yes.'

This rings a bell with Ludvík.

'Standa,' says Broken Nose. He stands to attention.

'Corporal Stanislav Chroust, Comrade Second Lieutenant!'

In the background of their meeting a group of specially productive workers is lining up for a photograph.

'Comrade Cibulka!' the organiser calls out.

'Present!'

'You'll be sitting on this chair. Don't go anywhere now. Madame Comrade Kopáčková!'

'Present.'

'Sit yourself here. The Comrade will be seated in this armchair. You'll be next to the Comrade.'

'Could I buy some more pictures later?'

'Most definitely.'

Droplets of sweat are forming on the organiser's forehead. He keeps on wiping them away with a handkerchief.

A banner hangs above the top row. With a message. Soldiers are holding it up on poles. The soldiers can be seen from the front.

'The biggest turn-up for the books was when we went to Ratškovice!' Broken Nose recalls. 'Remember it? Taking a tank to the village dance.'

'Yes, yes.'

'Do you want to try a shot of this? Good as a stick of dynamite. Real grapeshot! A payload like this has never yet been down the hatch!'

'She's looking for me... my wife...!' says Ludvík.

He looks around. He would like most of all to be able to free himself from this chap. Broken Nose is the sort to attach himself and never let go.

'No problem,' he says. 'Come with me. I know where she isn't going to find you.'

'But I... I must... I would like to speak with the Comrade.'

'Gone. Not here anymore. It would be one of the deadly sins not to drink this little number,' Stanislav says.

'The Comrade has left? But just now he was here.'

'Yes. And now he's gone away.'

Ludvík takes a closer look at Stanislav. He cannot quite get clear in his mind what sort of man he is dealing with. Where does he get his information from?

The spotlights are already on for the group of specially productive workers.

Someone is trying to add shading to the lights with bits of fabric.

Everyone is pushing their way forward.

'Comrade Volhrábek!' the organiser of the other group calls out.

'Left.'

'Left? How come he's left?'

Someone pushes forward to the organiser and whispers some explanation to him.

Discreetly he drops a hint by tilting a glass. Then stiffening up.

Meanwhile Stanislav has pulled Ludvík towards a door.

The one for staff. Out of which waiters emerge bearing trays and platters.

They go into a corridor. Away from the reception behind the scenes. It's full of cardboard boxes and crates. Trolleys stacked with clean and dirty dishes. They pass through the servery area. Where young women are putting the finishing touches to canapés. Where drinks are being poured and desserts set out on trays.

'Do you see that one, Ludo? The one with the melons? I tell you she'd bring tears to your eyes. She'd suck you dry.'

Between the kitchens there's a kind of bar area. A row of muscle is seated here, exactly ten strong.

'Boys, this is my platoon commander.'

Ludvík doesn't know them, but he recognises them.

One of the fellows has unbuttoned his jacket. Ludvík eyes his pistol. Suspended from artfully placed straps a little above the waist.

He offers everyone his hand and introduces himself.

Ludvík can't understand a word of the mumbled introductions from the men.

'With us you're better hidden away than the state's gold reserves, Ludo,' laughs Stanislav.

They've placed a carboy of unusual shape on the table. A product of remarkable craftsmanship.

'Do you know how old it is? Older than we are!'

'The archbishop was more desperate to keep this plum brandy than his diocese,' says one of them.

'Plum brandy should be old, but women should be young!'

'In the name of the Father, the Son and the Holy Spirit,' says Stanislav.

Everyone knocks back a drink.

'Ah!...' Ludvík cannot hold back a whoop of delight. 'This is worth an indulgence or two!'

The men fall about laughing. They like the joke.

Stanislav gives Ludvík another friendly cuff round the collarbone.

'This is our leading prankster,' he says. 'Our greatest puller of legs.'

Another round of drinks is ready.

Ludvík raises his glass. 'And so we all went off and happily married,' he says. With a sigh in place of a toast. 'And that was the end of us!'

Everyone starts yelling.

He's tapped into the right mood. Shown himself to have the popular touch.

He takes his glass and drinks the contents down in one, just as they do.

The organiser comes from the photo shoot and pokes his nose into their gathering.

'The Comrade went somewhere?' he inquires. His eyes are bulging with panic.

'Did Willy escort the Comrade somewhere?'

'Yes,' one of them replies to him. 'To the Strahov district. He went to show the new ambassador Prague by night.'

'But I have... the photography session all set up.'

'You're telling that to me?' asks another one built like a boulder.

'Am I supposed to get everyone to say "Cheese"?'

42

'You're leaving? Going somewhere?'

'No... no.'

'I see you've got a... dispatch case?'

Ludvík realises that he has his briefcase with him.

He laughs.

'No, no... it's just that I didn't know... there was a ring at the door... might have been a colleague... forgot it here... his briefcase.'

'If you need to get anywhere in a hurry,' says Orangutan, 'We're at your disposal. We've got horses and a carriage.'

At this moment Anna appears on the scene.

Ludvík wants to prevent any misunderstanding:

'The young men dropped off our keys,' he says. Trying to speak in a matter-of-fact way.

'You left them behind in the cloakroom!' he says. 'I thought that was the most likely place... the cloakroom. This is a friend of mine from military service. Standa.' He points to Stanislav. Who once again is being held up by two versions of Hercules.

'Didn't I tell you about him...?'

'No, you didn't.'

'When you hoist the flag,' says Stanislav, 'everyone stands... to attention! Whoever cannot stand may lie down but they must lie to attention by keeping their arms rigid!

'We were in Libavá together...'

'We chased pussy!'

'You idiot!' They start kicking him. 'Idiot,' they repeat to Stanislav.

'Stop yelling!'

Orangutan turns to Anna.

He offers her his hand.

He introduces himself. 'Podestálka is my name!'

Someone splutters in amusement.

They all introduce themselves.

Anna has to pass the little tube containing lighter fuel which she has brought for Ludvík from her right hand to her left.

One of them even introduces himself as Robinson Boozoe!

The one who looks as if he has a bit of brain left says to Anna: 'He's had a bit too much.'

'Who's had too much? Who? Me? Shall I sing you the national anthem?' He starts to sing: 'Where is my homeland?'

Someone begins to throttle him.

'If it's not too much trouble, Brother Comrade and Madame Comrade, might we ask you for a little coffee? For Standa here. So that we can get him into... an upright position.'

'But of course! Come in... comrades! We have plenty of coffee...'

'I don't know if we've got enough,' says Anna.

She has got over her earlier shock.

'I don't drink coffee,' shouts Stanislav. 'Coffee makes me puke, comrades! Do you have any tea? Did you know I was a minge drinker... binge drinker... tea-totaller?'

Again they start throttling him.

'Hold your tongue,' they say while Stanislav gets a kicking. 'Shut your gob.'

'You're kicking my ankle!'

'Come in, comrades.' Ludvík leads the woodentops inside. To the garden. No one is any longer to be seen by the summerhouse.

'It's not as if there's some blushing virgin among us,' says Stanislav in a low voice. He's picking a fight. Arguing with someone at the back of the group. 'Or is there a blushing virgin hiding somewhere?'

'Stop yelling! Idiot! His bit of skirt's here.'

Anna hears this from the front of the house.

Everyone hears it.

Anna looks at Ludvík.

Ludvík makes out that he hasn't heard anything.

'For starters I had to climb through the window of the laundry-room. Then I had to get to the kitchen, where we keep the spare keys.'

He's explaining all this to Orangutan.

Walking in the flowerbeds.

While Orangutan hogs the narrow path.

'I cannot appear at a social event, my friends, wearing shorts!' says Stanislav. 'Don't you... my friends, do not take this badly. There's no doubt about it!' The trousers he rolled up he now wants to roll down.

Which is enough to make him fall face forward into the dense shrubbery.

They are already at the house.

The door's wide open.

The visitors are bathed in light.

'Shoes off!' says Brains. 'Let's not bring any dirt to our lady comrade's clean floors.'

They all remove their shoes on the doorstep.

'Rudla!' they say to one of the group. 'In your case please keep them on!'

'Come right in... to the room...!' Obliging but still anxious, Ludvík invites them in.

He puts the briefcase right behind the door. On an easy chair.

'No! No! We can sit anywhere!' says Hulk. 'We're just ordinary folks...! We'll sit in the kitchen, with Comrade Madame's permission. We're not official guests!'

They stream into the kitchen in their socks.

Ludvík swiftly clears about a hundred things away from the table. He wipes away a spot with his sleeve. 'Annie...!' He is calling to Anna, who is a long way from being as obliging as Ludvík. 'Couldn't you pop a cloth onto the table!'

'The linen's in the laundry.'

'Even so... we still have a tablecloth...?'

'We haven't got one.'

He turns to the men. The brief exchange of words between himself and Anna has gone unnoticed.

'Sit down! Sit down!' he urges.

First of all they sit Stanislav down. He wastes no time in tumbling off his chair.

They put him back onto it.

He topples over the other side of the chair.

'Hold on! Hold onto the table!' they tell him.

Stanislav catches hold of the table.

'Ludo...!' he blinks up at Ludvík. 'You're not angry with me, are you? Ludo? We haven't disturbed you, have we, Madame Comrade?' He turns to Anna. 'We've met before, haven't we?'

'I don't know how we could have,' says Anna. All the same she takes another look at his mangled nose.

'Annie, would you put some coffee on, please?' asks Ludvík hastily.

Anna grabs the coffee pot and plonks it noisily on the stove. She makes no effort to hide her irritation. She switches on the electric hotplate.

'And if you could just fetch... I've got it upstairs... in my wardrobe there's some cognac... I brought it from Moscow the last time I was there...!'

Ludvík becomes aware of the keys in the palm of his hand. Hangs them on a hook. The very place where he was looking for them when he got back from the reception.

Anna has already gone out. Banging the door.

'Ludo...,' says Stanislav. 'The madame comrade... she's your lady?' He speaks quietly. 'The one that used to come and see you in our army days? Isn't that right?'

'Yes...'

Ludvík puts cognac glasses in front of everyone.

He takes them from the dresser, examines each one in turn, giving it a wipe with a dishcloth.

'I remember how she kept coming to see you...!' says Stanislav. 'Once we had to go chasing you... in a jeep! You were with that String Along!'

Colossus gives Stanislav another kick.

'What are you kicking me for? What have I said? I know the proper way to speak in company. I haven't been using any French words, have I?'

'Pull yourself together! All right?' says Orangutan. 'Just pull yourself together!'

'Can we light up?' asks Brains.

'Of course!'

'We'll be off in no time!' says Orangutan.

Ludvík puts an ashtray on the table for them.

Stanislav looks at the glass which Ludvík has placed in front of him.

'Do we have to keep filling our insides with drink, Comrades?' He heaves a sigh.

Suddenly he grows pale. Stands up. Holds on to the table.

It's clear to see that he's holding back the contents of his stomach.

'Have you got here... somewhere... Ludo... a plumbing network ... I've got an urgent package to send... by pneumatic tube.'

44

'We've got a loo here... downstairs. But it's blocked. Can you hold the package... till we get upstairs?'

'Relax, Ludo! ... Calm yourself!'

Ludvík propels Stanislav up the stairs. Ludvík has to support his back so that he doesn't topple backwards. Even so his foot seems unable to connect with the next stair.

'You won't have forgotten... how I went looking for you that time in the jeep? Remember? How she turned up and we kept her at the sentry post and you were with that String Along...'

'Pipe down,' says Ludvík.

'Of course!' says Stanislav. 'Wouldn't breathe a word to anyone...! This is all... just between ourselves.'

At last they get to the top.

Stanislav bends forward to be close to Ludvík's ear.

'I've got one too... Ludo... her indoors, an alligator.'

He puts on a woeful expression.

'I too have... my octopus!'

He breathes into Ludvík's face.

They've reached the toilet.

Ludvík opens the door for Stanislav. Puts the light on for him. Shuts the door behind him.

Anna emerges from the study.

As a meaningful gesture she puts the bottle of cognac on the floor.

'Once again I've been conned by you,' she says. In a cold fury she lowers her voice. 'Don't start telling me that you didn't invite them. Just don't say it. How could they have known, please answer me that...! How could they have known these were our keys? How? Don't you have any idea? From the keyring? They could tell bugger all from that. You were the one who checked out my cape. You took the keys out of my pocket and gave them to that... rumaholic! Once again you tricked your half-wit, Annie. Saying they were coming to take you in. They need to be taken in themselves! They came to drink us dry. They're the type to down litres.

'He's in the loo...! He can hear you!' he points out to Anna.

'Why do you think I'm saying all this? I want him to hear. I remember his mug only too well! I remember it from when I was visiting you during your army service. He was always pulling the wool over my eyes even then. You've found your-self a right friend there again. Isn't Cejnar enough for you?'

Anna goes to the bedroom. Slams the door behind her. Straight away locks the door from the inside.

'Annie!' Ludvík grabs hold of the handle.

He runs to the study. To the connecting door with the bedroom.

But Anna has already locked this door too from the bedroom side. Ludvík rattles the handle to no avail.

Now Stanislav has flushed the loo and is opening the door.

'Ludo!'

Ludvík comes out of the study.

Stanislav looks in surprise at the bottle of cognac.

'Is this a bottle that I see before me, the screw-top toward my hand? On the floor? Or is it but a ghost?' He points at it.

'It is a bottle!'

Ludvík picks up the bottle. He stands it on the side table.

Stanislav closes the door and at the same time leans on it. Which means it is at once open again.

This time Ludvík shuts the door.

'Was your privy struck by a thunderbolt? How did you get your throne to burn like that?'

'Do you want to wash your hands?'

He guides Stanislav to the bathroom. Moves to pick up scattered articles of underwear left by Anna. Throws them behind the bath. Turns the tap on for Stanislav. Gets him a towel.

Stanislav puts his head under the running water.

'Ludo... I think I've left... my jacket... in there!'

It's true that he isn't wearing a coat. Ludvík realises that now. Goes into the corridor. Opens the door to the loo. Picks the jacket up off the floor. Sleeves inside out. Puts them the right way round. In disgust. Then becomes aware of his warm sweater. Removes his jacket. Removes the sweater and flings it somewhere. Puts the jacket back on. Returns to the bathroom.

Where Stanislav is already in front of the mirror attacking a thick mop of stripy hair – a sure sign of a healthy but empty head – with half of a small comb.

45

'Drink up,' mumbles Orangutan. Talking to Stanislav. Who's sipping coffee.

'Get it down you! You're tippling like a teenage girl. The comrade deputy minister wants to get some shut-eye.'

'It's all right, lads,' says Ludvík. 'No hurry. In Australia it's only half-past eight in the evening.'

He has taken off his jacket and rolled up the sleeves of his shirt. He seems calmer. Pours himself another glass.

'One for the road,' he says. 'And another one to find the right road.'

The kitchen is full of cigarette smoke. One bottle stands empty in the middle of the table. The gherkin jar is half empty too. A single schnitzel has survived on the plate. Alongside the remains of some roast and a quarter of a sliced cake. Bread, knife, a few forks and some packets of cigarettes which Ludvík retrieved from his pockets are strewn across the plastic tablecloth.

'I am not going to cripple my kisser just for your sake,' Stanislav tells Orangutan. 'Come on!'

Taking hold of their glasses, they all rise to their feet. Even those who've been sitting on the floor manage to rise. They've got cushions from somewhere. Probably from the hall.

'Better to come up than to go down,' says Muscles. His meaning unclear.

'Cheers!' says Brains. 'Bottoms up!'

'And off we go! Ready for a ride!'

They surge out of the kitchen in their socks.

There's a drunken *mêlée* in the doorway as they push into one another.

Ludvík presses upon them another two full bottles which he has prepared beforehand.

'Oh no! Comrade... we couldn't possibly accept them.'

'Don't be silly, lads!'

They stuff the bottles into their pockets.

'Cigarettes! Grab some cigarettes!'

These too go into their pockets.

Ludo is... a class act!' mutters Stanislav. 'I told you he was... one of the boys to his fingertips!'

They tackle their laces on the steps.

Stanislav battles to get his feet into lace-ups. Tramples down the backs of the shoes with his heels. Doesn't see what he's doing. Puts on his shoes as if they were slippers.

Once again, his trouser legs find their way above his knees.

Off they go along the concrete pathway...

They reach the gate.

Ludvík casts a watchful eye around him once again.

Orangutan notices this.

Catches up with Ludvík. Looks at him.

'Should you see some people hanging around here,' he says, 'they'll be ours.'

He speaks to Ludvík from close up. Keeps it between themselves.

'We had things to do at the house next door. Where Klepáč lives. You heard about that, Comrade, didn't you?'

'It's Ludo to you,' says Ludvík. 'Seeing that we're on first-name terms. 'Yes,' he adds, 'I did hear that...'

'Maybe there's still a security patrol here ... hanging around.'

Orangutan takes a look round.

'You didn't see anyone? In the garden?'

'No one. In the garden, you say?' He affects indifference. Steels himself to keep looking Hulk in the eyes.

'Maybe the lads have wrapped up early,' says Muscle in surprise.

He stands on the pathway.

While they are going out. They have the car windows open. They are calling to Ludvík.

He replies to them in the same tone of voice.

'Be seeing you, lads!'

Stanislav sticks his leg out of the window right up to the knee. He loses a half-laced shoe.

'Stop! Stop, you idiots!'

Ludvík runs up and passes the shoe into the car.

Once more they set off. And are gone.

He turns round. Goes back in at the gate. Whistles on and off. Locks up. Goes along the concrete path. Back towards home.

Steps into the vegetable patch where the radishes are. Picks one.

Wipes it on his trousers. Munches it.

Flings the haulm into the shrubbery.

46

The group for the photograph has wilted from waiting.

The men smoke. The women chatter. The banner leans against the wall. Behind the back row of the cast the soldiers are sitting. Between the oleanders.

'No moving apart!' the organiser calls out.

'Ludo!' says Cejnar. 'These are the prettiest girls from Broumov.'

He introduces Ludvík to three of the specially productive workers. They seem quite young. Bulging in their sweaters and with big red hands.

They are giggling. Holding onto the bumpkin bags of country life as if they were life belts. One has a dress with a fur border round the neck.

'Aren't they well-built? Don't think it's just scaffolding propping them up inside!'

The women manage to titter sheepishly.

'Vlasta! Give Ludvík the rule of honour!'

'No moving apart!' the organiser reminds the women. 'The Comrade is coming! The Comrade is coming now!'

Vlasta is the woman with the fur. She produces a leather case from her bag. Inside it is a bricklayer's one-metre folding rule. Painted gold.

'We brought this to you from Broumov, Comrade Deputy Minister, so that you... so that you...'

She doesn't finish. She turns to two of her companions. There is an outburst of giggling.

'So that you can measure whatever you need to measure at home when you have a moment to spare,' says Cejnar.

'Don't grab it too tightly. The paint will come off.'

The heads of the women huddle together as they fail to hold back their laughter.

'Who is this lady comrade?'

'She's from Nušovice,' says Cejnar. 'A bundle of laughs. Her man got taken in. On account of opening his mouth too much. Now we've finally twisted her arm enough to get her to divorce him. You should come and see us! Besides, we've got some building work that still needs approval, it's way overdue! We must do something about that. It's all happening in Nusovice...'

47

He is still whistling when he reaches the kitchen.

Anna is standing by the fridge. She has opened all the windows in the kitchen. She is wearing crumpled flannel pyjamas. Nothing on her feet. Her figure is even more shapeless without underwear. She's drinking mineral water. Pouring it into a glass.

'You had to give them the cake too?'

Her voice is calm for the moment.

'Nothing was too good for them! Even the cake I baked for our anniversary. You stuffed it down the throats of a bunch of drunks.'

Ludvík goes up to Anna.

'Forget the cake,' he says.

He gives a sigh of relief: 'That was a close call. Thank the Lord!'

He takes the bottle of mineral water from Anna's hand and drinks directly from the bottle.

'Don't drink from the bottle. If I do that you have a fit.'

'That's something you just can't understand. The fact that you're meant to be a lady.'

'Perhaps I could understand better if you treated me like one.'

He closes the windows.

'Clean it yourself. I wouldn't even touch it. I wouldn't even think of cleaning it.'

'I wouldn't even expect you to. I know perfectly well that if I wanted to eat dinner on a clean plate, I'd have to go and buy the plate first.' Ludvík drags a table that's overflowing with untidiness across the lino and up to the door of the pantry. He opens the door. Goes to the other side of the table and shoves it inside.

The table just about fits inside the pantry. Taking up all the space between the shelves.

He closes the door.

'Done and dusted!' he says. 'And I'll get you a pair of cakes in the morning.'

He kisses Anna's neck. 'Go and get into your gear,' he whispers.

His hand creeps under her flannel pyjamas and starts to explore.

Anna wrenches herself free.

'I'm not in the mood for that right now! Turning myself into a geisha for a night like Madame Butterfly! You amaze me! How can you be in the mood for something like that? What did they say about Košara? And about Klepáč?'

Ludvík is pulling a shaggy carpet from the hall to the kitchen.

To the free space created by moving the table.

He pushes the chairs next to the wall.

'Nothing... what would you expect them to say?'

A bed sheet is stuffed behind the cushions of an armchair in the hall. It doesn't look clean or as if it has seen an iron recently.

Ludvík unfolds the sheet over the shaggy carpet.

'Don't bother setting up,' says Anna. 'I've got a headache.'

Ludvík adds some pillows to the makeshift bed.

'Do you want something for your head? We've got pills in the sideboard.'

'Didn't they tell you anything...? About why those two were lifted? You did ask them, didn't you...when you were all chatting together?'

'I'll bring you your things... all right? I'll nip and get them for you. Where did you put your nightie?'

Anna takes a long look at Ludvík. Without speaking.

'So you didn't even ask them?' she eventually says. She doesn't take her eyes away from him. 'You wouldn't even ask them if I was the one lifted! Won't one of you at least ask about Košara? About what's happened to him? You could at least have asked. Couldn't you?'

Ludvík closes the door to the hall.

'Don't shut the door. Ear can listen in, for all I care. We're forever closing doors. Not even the gypsies have to use the kitchen for nookie. And on the floor at that! Even the Hottentots have moved beyond that.'

'Nor do we have to do this! We can stay in the bedroom! Shall we stay in the bedroom?' asks Ludvík.

It's clear that he doesn't like the campsite set-up that much either.

Anna gives a sigh.

'Forget it! You might not care about having your bedroom thrills recorded...! It matters to me!'

Anna opens the door to the pantry. She's alone in the kitchen now.

She turns on the light. Looks through the clutter on the table for a cigarette. Has to sift through several empty packets. Finally finds one. Finds matches too. Lights the cigarette.

Bare of foot and baggy of pyjama, she makes her way back to the chair. Sits down and drags another chair closer with a foot before resting both feet on it.

This is the moment when Ludvík enters. Stripped down to a pair of tight-fitting trunks.

Across his arm he carries a black night slip for Anna. And a fur. And high heels.

'They'll have to let Košara's wife go!' says Anna. 'If they've taken her in, they'll have to let her go. After all, she's got kids.'

'Kids!' says Ludvík. 'What do you think we're dealing with here, the Red Cross?'

He puts the slip and fur around Anna's shoulder and the shoes into her lap.

'Where would she put them? It's not as if Košara's wife has any family in Prague.'

'They'll dump them somewhere....! That'll be the least of their problems.'

Even Ludvík finds his way to the pantry and searches for a cigarette amidst the débris on the table.

'None left!' says Anna. 'I tracked down the last one.' She holds out her hand. 'Here!'

She offers him hers.

Ludvík takes it and inhales greedily.

'Košara didn't want... the report submitted. The one about the brickworks. You didn't want to either at first. They made you... when they began to prepare that nasty resolution against you. Saying you were not up to the job and should leave the ministry. You ought to tell someone. Lay it on the line. Explain this was why you backed the report'.

'It's not easy to explain!' says Ludvík. It's not a subject he likes brought up. 'We could be talking about this until morning.'

'We might as well talk,' she says. 'After all, we can't sleep.'

'For Christ's sake, do I have to go on about this even with you? With everyone else and then you into the bargain? Do I concern myself with the state of your saucepans?'

She goes silent for a while.

'You shouldn't have said that.'

Anna gets up and goes to the kitchen dresser. Hunts among the cups.

'Where have I put my pills?' she asks in a different tone of voice. 'Have you seen my pills anywhere?'

'I haven't taken them,' says Ludvík. 'The pills don't work on me anymore.'

'Don't play the martyr. How many times have I been lying awake while you've been sleeping like a log!'

But she doesn't care about the point she's making. She's already found her little box of pills.

It wasn't in the dresser. It was among the spice boxes. On a shelf.

Above the stove.

Anna taps out a few pills onto her palm. Gulps them down and throws a look of contempt at Ludvík.

'Why do you look at me like that? What can I know of why they were pulled in? Did I turn Košara in? Is that what you think? It could just as well have been me they came for! I could have been the one stuck in a cell. As if I knew how they decide who to lift and when.'

'Except that it's Košara they've taken in and you they've come to party with!'

Ludvík's jaw drops.

'Have you gone mad?'

'Too right I have.'

Anna goes to the pantry. Takes an unfinished bottle from the mess on the table. It's cognac. Wipes the top with her pyjama sleeve. And drinks.

'Yesterday it was ten years since I went out of my mind. I'll drink to that now.'

She uses the two chairs to sit down again. Places the bottle on the floor. Within reach.

'Why must you always pretend to be something you're not in front of me? I know you well enough. If I'd wanted a saint or a genius, I dare say I'd have married someone else. My bad luck was that I wanted you...'

'I'll tell you something,' says Ludvík. 'You know what...?'

'Yes, I know!' she says. 'I shouldn't be finishing this bottle. Because it's not a pedagogically sound thing to do... when I'm in a drunken condition and have to get Ludi ready for school. I already know everything you've said to me over the last ten years by heart. It's not so much to remember! All of ten sentences!'

'Get off my back!' he says.

'That's one!' she says. 'You've nine sentences to go.'

He turns sharply and goes out of the kitchen.

'Wait!' she shouts. She jumps up and hurries over to him. He stops. She holds out her hand.

'Leave the cigarette here with me. It's mine.'

49

She sits in the kitchen for a while longer. She draws up her legs and rests her chin on her knees. The fur and the slip she chucks onto the nearest chair.

She smokes the cigarette right down to the end. Until she burns her fingers. Then stubs it out on the bottle. Leans back, throws the butt behind the rib-shaped radiator. Gets up. Goes into the hall. To the telephone. Lifts the receiver. Quickly dials some number.

It rings for a long time before a male voice materialises at the end of the phone. 'Who am I speaking to?'

Anna doesn't reply. Hangs up.

'Who were you calling? What are you doing fooling around?'

Ludvík is standing at the top of the stairs.

She turns to face him.

'I was trying to call... Košara's wife,' she explains. 'Some bloke was there.'

'Obviously. He'll have used the other phone line to ring the switchboard. So he could trace the number that was calling. By now they'll think I was ringing Košara.'

'They won't,' she says. 'Ear knows what we're doing. Why should you have made a call? When you know he's been... taken in?'

Ludvík lowers his voice.

'Officially they told me nothing. I got to know what was happening... by chance. No one ever called me about it. No one spoke to me. What a great help you've been!'

She purses her lips. Picks up the receiver again. Holds it to her ear. 'Put it down!' Ludvík says to her. 'Put it down!'

She's already dialled the number.

Ludvík rushes down the stairs. Straight to Anna.

But he's too late to wrench the receiver from her grasp. The voice is already on the other end of the line:

'Who am I speaking to?'

Ludvík hears it too.

The sound fills the hall.

'It wasn't my husband ringing a moment ago!' says Anna.
In a voice with a hint of unease in it.

'I was the one calling.'

50

Two men enter by the connecting gate, in the pale half-light that envelops the shrubbery, the ancient brickwork and the blurred silhouettes of the garden trees. They carry a long ladder across their shoulders, holding it flat as they drag it along.

They don't act like people who are good with their hands. They don't have the hang of working with tools.

Anna watches them from the bedroom window as they try to manoeuvre themselves somewhere behind the house. They haven't judged the length of the ladder correctly and a young tree gets in the way as they make a turn.

The men in the garden argue about it.

'Why would they bring a ladder from the Klepáč place to here?' asks Anna. Ludvík is removing a pillow, duvet and sheet from the bedroom and taking them to the study next door. He is not going to sleep in the bedroom but on a couch in the next room.

'Stop taking any notice of it, I tell you. It doesn't concern us. It's for... the security squad.'

She turns round.

'What?'

'They've got... things they have to do. After all, gardens are passageways...! On all sides. There's yet another gate here...the one leading to the Froněks' place.'

'You mean Froněk has something to do with this?'

'I don't know. But after all he was with Tondl... in the same department... his maiden name was Jewish – Friedmann...'

Anna doesn't get the point.

'What's that? What do you mean?'

Ludvík doesn't explain to her. He's in the study. He returns for a moment.

'Could you tell me where my pyjamas are? Could you at least suggest their rough whereabouts...?'

'Where you put them is where you'll find them.'

'Are we still a household? Or have we become something else?'

'So you spoke to them about it?'

Ludvík kneels down and looks under the bed. Inside the wardrobe. Checks every chair.

'You've always lied to me,' says Anna. She is lying on the bed. 'I've never got the truth out of you. Always had to find out what was going on from strangers.'

Ludvík goes to her bed. Lifts up her pillow even with her head on it.

His pyjamas are not underneath the pillow. Instead there's an open box of Anna's chocolates.

'You won't find anything in my bed! You took them off in the bathroom, didn't you?'

'There's nothing in the bathroom.'

'Take clean ones, then. There's some in the briefcase. I packed it for you when you were being taken in. The briefcase is in the hall downstairs.'

Anna switches off her bedside light.

The bedroom is in semi-darkness. Light comes from the open door to the study. And from the half-open door to the landing.

'You were already lying to me in Mohelnice. You were lying when we still had the business... I never even knew that you'd gone through all that money... If Dad hadn't told me you'd never have said a word about it...! Or in Olomouc! You were full of how Košara needed you in Prague, and all along it was about someone who didn't want you in Olomouc.'

Ludvík comes back into the bedroom. He turns the radio on. It's standing on the bedside table. He has it on because of Ear.

'Are we going to sleep? Or will you go on talking like a book?'

'You can close the door. I'm just talking to myself.'

'You know who talks out loud to themselves, don't you?'

'The Comrade does.'

He turns up the radio.

'Košara didn't come to win you over! He came to rescue you! He took you to the ministry with him because the bureau had you up against a wall! Goodness knows who else had you up against a wall...'

She sits up. In the bed.

'Even Košara was spooked by you. Did you know...?'

Ludvík searches through her bag. Tracks down cigarettes. And a lighter. Lights up. Sits down on a chair in his trunks. Next to the radio.

'You must have spent a long time working all that out. Did you manage it on your own? You must have spent as much time thinking about it as Božena Němcová spent writing her masterpiece.'

Ludvík is not as calm as he seems. He taps the ash from his cigarette into a vase of plastic flowers.

'Klepáč didn't like you either!' says Anna.

Ludvík turns off the radio.

Anna doesn't notice this.

'Klepáč was a clever fellow. Wrote books. Why do you think he never invited us? Not once, throughout the two years we've been here! Ever thought why that might be? After all, his wife used to live in my pocket! Klepáč was also afraid of you. Saw through you. Had your number from the very beginning.'

This is the moment when Anna realises Ludvík has turned off the radio.

She glances at the radio. Glances at Ludvík.

'Why don't you turn on some music... for Ear?' she asks.

Then she realises. Opens her mouth.

Ludvík stands up. Heads for the door to the study.

'Do you know why everyone's afraid of you? Do you know why? They know you'd use their corpses as stepping-stones to get what you want.'

He shuts the door.

Anna addresses her words to the closed door.

'All you're concerned about is yourself,' she shouts. 'You don't care about anyone else. When your own interests are at stake, you don't even look after your own kith and kin!'

She pauses for breath.

'Not even your own brother!' she says. 'You wrote your brother out of your resumé. Because he'd been in England and because...'

Suddenly he has the door open. He's running. Almost trips on the carpet by the bed.

Quick as a flash Anna buries her head under the duvet. Frantically holds it over her head with both hands.

While Ludvík tries with all his might to rip the duvet away from her.

Anna kicks out with her legs. A few times she actually kicks Ludvík.

She cries out from under the duvet: 'He's hitting me! He's hitting me again!' She screams: 'Help! Comrades, help! This is battery!'

Ludvík has no choice but to climb across both beds on his knees. As far as the radio. He puts it on full volume. 'I'll show you!' he says in a hoarse voice. 'Just you wait...!'

She makes use of the moment. Jumps up. Runs out of the bedroom.

Ludvík hurries after her.

Anna wants to lock herself inside the loo.

But Ludvík gets there first. His leg is in the doorway. His strength is too much for her. Slowly the door gives way. Until it's open.

'What's that?' he says to Anna, his face close to hers. 'Do you want me to sock you in the mouth? Is that what you want – a smack in the gob?'

Anna is holding the plunger in her hand. As a weapon.

Ludvík grabs hold of her wrist and twists.

The light is on in the loo.

He has closed the door.

They are both panting.

'Another thing you never put in the resumé – that you gave lectures on Masaryk...!'

'Stop this!'

'There wasn't a dry eye in the house!'

'Stop this, I tell you!'

'And what a good dancer you were. How beautifully you cut a caper in the folk costume of the Kyjov region all the way from the station to the Hotel Beránek when President Beneš came to Mohelnice...'

He has wrenched the plunger free from Anna's grip. Throws it into the toilet bowl. Anna is furious and spits in his face.

Ludvík slaps her across the face.

This doesn't surprise her in any way.

'And how you sang! After régime change, when it was Comrade Gottwald's turn to visit. You spent the whole night singing patriotic songs. Until you lost your voice!'

Ludvík is pulling the chain to flush the loo.

This gives Anna an opportunity and she opens the door of the lavatory.

'You were in our version of the Hitler Youth under the German occupation... you were in the Sokol gymnastics organisation... you were on your knees as an altar boy... it's all the same to you... find whatever bandwagon's rolling and clamber on to get as far as you can.'

Swiftly he shuts the door. Has his hands under Anna's neck. Almost strangles her.

Blood flows from Anna's nose down to her upper lip.

She feels it there and uses her tongue to lick her lips.

'So hit me then! What's making you hesitate, Comrade? After all, you know how to do it, don't you?'

She leans her head against the wall.

'If I was a ladybird, you'd be tearing off my little wings, wouldn't you? You'd be mashing me to a pulp.'

The blood on Anna's nose brings Ludvík back to his senses a little.

'You start drinking... you get drunk! Then you don't have any idea what you're rattling on about.'

'You're wrong. I know very well what I'm rattling on about. You're glad that I drink!'

'Haven't you got a handkerchief? Isn't there one in your pyjamas?'

He holds on to her hands with one of his own while searching through the little pockets of her flannel pyjamas with his other hand. No handkerchief there. Just the usual thing that women tend to have in the pockets of their pyjamas. And that's the last thing these two need right now.

'That's what you're counting on... my drinking myself to death...! Or drinking myself silly, so that one fine day you can dump me in some loony-bin! Giving you a free hand! That's how things are done... among the comrades! In the footsteps of comrade Stalin...'

He covers her mouth. Getting blood on his palm. He gets blood all over her face.

As she struggles against him.

'Please... stop... making a fool of yourself!'

But the menace has gone out of Ludvík's voice. On the contrary. It grows cajoling.

He opens the door of the loo with his elbow. Keeps hold of Anna by the mouth with one hand. Grips her hand with the other. Holding it behind her back.

Apparently causing her pain. Forcing her to comply.

He directs her firmly into the bathroom.

'Time and again it's me who has to get your brother out of a jam. Who lent a hand to pull him out of the mire? I did! He'd have been stuck in gaol till he turned blue if I hadn't been able to get him out.'

The first thing Ludvík does is lock the door.

Anna struggles against him while he tries to push her over to the washbasin.

'If you hadn't pulled him out of the mire, he'd still be sitting in it. But you also wouldn't be sitting where you're sitting now. Don't turn yourself into a Francis of Assisi. Don't make out that you ever do something for the sake of some-body else. Your decency is always just a matter of s-h-o-w.'

He keeps dragging her towards the tap.

She clings to the door handle, while he hacks at her arm. Painfully.

'You're not going to put cold water on my neck!' yells Anna. 'I'll have a blocked nose for ten days!'

'Do you want to be dripping blood till morning? Is that what you'd prefer? Remember what the bed looked like last time.'

Ludvík is already running the water.

Anna uses her free hand to turn off the tap.

Ludvík turns it on again. And pays more attention to her free hand.

'Lean forward! Let's do this the easy way. The hard way will hurt you.'

Anna tries to kick Ludvík. With her knee. Her face already looks as if she's in business as a butcher.

'You shit!' she swears. 'You complete shit!'

'Is that the teacher in you speaking?' asks Ludvík. 'You were a teacher for all of three days, weren't you! Until they sent you packing! What a sight! Just take a look at yourself!'

He lifts Anna's head so she can see herself in the mirror. She looks terrible.

'Take a look! Take a look at yourself!'

'That's it,' she says. Looks at herself. 'That's what I look like after ten years here with you!'

'So why did you marry me? Why get hitched up with such a crook?'

'I could spend a long time explaining why I married you. But you'd never understand. Do you know why? Because there are certain things missing in you that only normal people have. But I can easily tell you why you married me....! Stop twisting my arm! Stop it!'

'I will when you bend forward! Bend forward!'

'My hair will get wet! My pyjamas will be completely soaked!'

'If you don't lean forward, I'll break your arm.'

'Why didn't you marry Jitka? What a love affair that was! And Jitka was still a virgin. Shall I tell you? Why you didn't marry her? And why you hooked up with me?'

'As if I haven't heard this a dozen times already!'

They continue to battle ferociously, though keeping the noise down.

'As for me, I'd gone to bed with a whole football team. You knew that perfectly well. A whole football team – apart from you. Do you remember when I did go to bed with you? It was when Jirka didn't turn up for a date. There came a point when each one of them would just stop showing up. Off they went and married some other girl.'

'Shut up! Can't you just hold your tongue for once?'

In a barefoot battle each tries to trip the other up. A bast mat slips from under them. They fall on their knees. Then on their stomachs.

Blood trickles down onto Anna's chin. It's now on her neck. And on her pyjamas.

When they reach ground level, they're surrounded by what you'd expect to see in bathrooms. A waste bin. Scales and sweat-stained slippers swollen by their stretched insides. Soap that has fallen onto the floor tiles. Ludvík finds himself looking at the bath for a moment. There among all the clutter he'd piled into it he spots his pyjamas.

'You were such a terrible catch that I could've guessed you'd marry me. You had one pair of trousers, one jumper, socks that had been through darning. We had a pub. A house. Poor daddy kept telling anyone who'd listen that it would be worth a hundred thousand to be the other half and get the little slag married off.'

Ludvík slaps Anna once again.

'Will you hold your tongue? Will you...'

'All those boys... they were something. They weren't all clever. Some were stupid. But they were something. You were flavourless, nothing sweet and nothing savoury. You didn't have any mark to distinguish you. It took me ages when I was alone to remember what you looked like. Average height, average weight, average schooling, average...'

He stands her up. Grabs Anna round the neck. And finally succeeds. Drives the top half of her body down towards the washbasin.

Anna writhes around while Ludvík uses all his strength to hold her down.

'Let me go! You shit!'

Ice-cold water streams over Anna's head. In this position she is defenceless. Ludvík now has one hand free.

He rinses Anna's face. As if he's bathing a small child.

Anna erupts with a 'Yuck!' and 'It's cold, you cretin!' Her hands try to grab hold of Ludvík.

But under the stream of water she can't see what she's doing.

He can easily keep her under control. He turns the tap to increase the flow.

'Ow!'

She whimpers.

'You swine...! ... You bastard! You didn't even pop Jitka's cherry... you coward! You didn't want to ruin your prospects... your chance to get the money... to set up a building firm... that's another thing you didn't write in your resumé! That you had a building company...! Turn off the water!'

'When you've finished your rant. When you've sobered up. When's that likely to be?'

She manages to hit Ludvík. Painfully.

In the most sensitive part of his body.

'I'll drown you. Got that? One of these days I'm going to drown you.'

'That'd be too much for someone like you. It's out of your league to do anything... special. You even ran that company of yours into the ground. You were so useless! Daddy had to give you an extra fifty thousand... and you still went arse up! You came a cropper! If things hadn't changed in '48, we'd have had nothing left. You couldn't even pull off a swindle. When you tried to work that scam over planks, they were on your tail at once... fortunately the February coup turned up in time and you moved into politics... but even in politics, where everyone's at the trough, your snout could hardly push its way through! Stop the water! I'm freezing already.'

Ludvík turns off the tap.

Anna remains for a while in the same position.

Ludvík is no longer holding her. She wrings the water out of her wet hair.

'Thanks to you there'll soon be nothing left in the trough for me,' says Ludvík. 'I don't lord it over people, you're the one who plays Lady Muck! Who's always got the car seat beneath her bum? Is it me? Is it? I don't have my own car even when I need it. Because you've always got it! Off in the car to the market, off in the car to the hairdresser, off in the car for a bit of botany picking lily of the valley. Do you think no one ever cottons on? In any case you let everyone know. When the drink loosens your tongue. About how you sent Jindřich to Budějovice for blueberries. But why did we never drive to see your father? Before he died? Why? Could you tell me that?'

Anna is looking at herself in the mirror.

'I'll look like a cow once more,' she says.

Ludvík moves so he's standing right next to her.

'You didn't want to go back to Mohelnice. In case someone was reminded that your family used to have a business. So no one could spoil our chances. That's something I did include in my resumé, you know. That you came from bourgeois stock. Do you think I'm getting some bonus for that?'

Ludvík drags Anna away from the basin to the bath. Sits her down on the side.

'Lean your head back', he says. 'The bleeding will stop right away.'

He is still treating Anna like a child.

He wets a towel, wrings out the water and puts it on Anna's forehead and nose.

Anna flings the towel onto the ground.

'Kindly don't swipe my face with the rags you use to dry your feet!'

53

'It's not as if your women mean anything to me,' says Anna. 'I don't give a toss about them. Not even about Konvičková.'

She is still leaning her head back.

'It isn't as if you could fall in love with any of them. Not even if she was the Queen of Sheba. You're only in love with yourself.'

'Amen!' says Ludvík. 'Is that the end of the sermon?'

He lifts a pile of clothes from behind the bath. Extracts his pyjamas. Throws Anna's things back. Without her noticing anything.

Anna doesn't even glance at Ludvík.

'The womanising began right after the wedding. As soon as I'd shown you the ropes. You began to pass on what you'd learned. Only everything calls for some talent. Even that needs talent. Which you don't have.'

'If I were you... I wouldn't be so sure of that.'

Ludvík keeps his voice down more than Anna. It's clear that he doesn't like speaking out loud about these things. If Anna hadn't wounded his pride, he would probably have said nothing.

'Besides, you don't even get a kick out of it with any of them... it's only with the halfwit Anna that it's anything but dull.'

'Go and lie down! Put a wet compress on your forehead. Do you have any idea what time it is now?'

'It's only half past eight in Australia,' says Anna. 'That was your second sentence. What makes you think I'll put up with this forever, this waiting for someone like you, the begging for more of nothing? You can get all that right out of your head.'

'Some sow their wild oats before marriage,' says Ludvík. 'Others need to drop some seeds after marriage. Nature always finds the correct balance. That's what Marxism tells us.'

Anna gets up and goes out of the door.

She goes to the corridor. To the chair which has a cup of cold coffee on it. Coffee which she originally brought for Ludvík. And which she now sips with disgust.

'Don't try to pass your filthy ideas off as holy writ. Don't think you're the only one. The only one who can play that game. I can do it too.'

'Just tell me one thing. Is this another occasion when we go on talking drivel till morning? Is it? Why don't you go and lie down?'

He looks out of the window.

The outline of the trees in the garden seems to be clearer.

'It will be getting light.'

'Do you remember Viktor? The one with the curly hair? The one who drove us around?'

Ludvík is looking for her handbag. In the bedroom. Tracks down a cigarette. Lights it.

'No,' he says. 'I don't remember.' He holds his head in his hands. 'I don't even remember how old I am. When I was born.'

'Sentence number three,' she says. 'It was when you were in Moscow with that government delegation. I spent those ten days teaching him mouth-to-mouth! Daily. And you know where we started? On the street. Right in front of the gate. In the car.'

'Anna.'

He reminds her that she's speaking out loud.

'Just let them get an earful... the comrades! They like hearing this. Better than hearing drivel from you. They need something to help them jerk off. Do you want to hear something else?'

'No. I've heard enough.' Ludvík is losing control of himself.

'At least I know what you did with all that money. That really must have cost you... a packet!'

For a moment Anna does no more than look at Ludvík.

First her lips start trembling. Then the whole of her chin. She blinks. And then unexpectedly she sends the contents of her mug spewing into his face. It is the moment when she loses her self-composure and bursts into tears.

The whole of her face erupts into a savage howl beyond control.

An explosion.

She moves away from Ludvík. Runs away.

But doesn't head for the bedroom. Hurries along the corridor to the staircase. Runs down the stairs to the hall.

Ludvík is still wiping his face with his sleeve. His first reflex is to pick up the mug from where she's thrown it on the carpet.

But instead he goes running after Anna.

'Anna!'

54

He catches up with her. Tries to hold her.

Grabs Anna by the sleeve. But Anna thrashes out at Ludvík furiously.

'What do you care about me? You don't care for me at all. Leave me alone.'

From the hall she heads for the steps down to the cellar. Knocks over a pot with her bare foot.

Ludvík zigzags around pots and pans as he follows her.

'Where are you going?'

'Down there.'

'Come and lie down. I'll sleep in the bedroom. I'll bring my stuff back! To the bedroom.'

'You needn't do me any favours. I'm not asking you for any. Does anyone want favours from you?'

Now they're in the cellar.

'You want to sleep in the cellar?'

'You bet! On your account I'll start sleeping in the cellar. As if you were worth it...'

She reaches down for a bowl with meat in it.

The one Ludvík brought down.

She turns round, moves past Ludvík and heads for the stairs taking the meat with her...

...as far as the kitchen.

She puts the bowl into the fridge. Slams shut the hefty door.

Heads for the sink. Which is surrounded by dirty dishes. Though the oldest of the dirty dishes have been shoved into a couple of washtubs.

Anna pulls them out and starts filling the sink with water. Sprinkles powder for washing dishes into the stream from the tap.

'You want to do the dishes right now?' asks Ludvík. 'For goodness' sake, the birds are already singing outside.'

'And the prick is singing inside,' says Anna in a tone of contempt as she lowers her voice.

'It's not as if it's Saturday, is it? Isn't Saturday the day for doing dishes?'

'Do you have to hang around here with your cackle? Cackle, cackle, all the time cackling?' Anna turns away and lifts the fur off the chair. Throws it round Ludvík's neck. Throws the nightie into his face. 'Go to bed. Don't worry about stupid Anna. She's no longer your Hawaiian dancing girl... no more naked antics... from now on the one thing I'll be is dutiful comrade Zoja.'

She squats down. In order to lift up a pyramid of plates. From the ground. The dishes are piled up everywhere under the sink. A good hundred plates!

And it is at this very moment, when she has grasped hold of an armful and lifted them up while still squatting on the floor, that she spots an unusual object at the foot of the sink.

Which immediately catches her eye.

It's a little black prism with lots of little holes. Lying on the lino.

Two insulated wire leads, as thin as hairs, issue from the prism. There are jack plugs at the end of each and

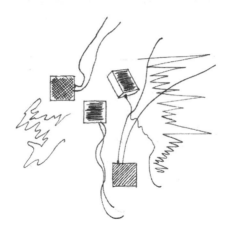

they're plugged in. The tiny openings are almost at the join between the floor and the wall. The holes look like they've always been there. They seem to belong to an outdated socket. The flat kind.

An old socket with several layers of paint.

'Ludo!' whispers Anna. 'Ludo!'

She turns to face Ludvík. Without moving from her squatting position. She doesn't even put down the plates. 'Look what I've found.'

Anna's expression, her tone of voice and the way she moves her head to beckon him over lead Ludvík to kneel down next to his wife.

Their heads are almost side by side.

They are surrounded by dirty dishes, a battered bucket of slops and a cardboard box full of pieces of stale bread.

Ludvík has already spotted the object.

'It wasn't here yesterday,' says Anna.

Ludvík puts his finger to his mouth with a meaningful glance. A signal that she should be quiet.

He wants to touch the object, reaches out with his hand towards the prism but then pulls his hand back again.

He takes the plates out of Anna's arms. Carefully puts them back where they were. Straightens himself up.

Anna stands up too.

Ludvík finds his breath again. Turns on the tap to run a noisy stream of water.

'That's...Ear,' he says.

'No!'

'Shhh!'

'They wouldn't put it... where we could find it. They'd have known we'd come across it.'

'When were the plumbers here?'

'Way back! Must be a month ago already. They must've known we'd find this thing.'

Anna gulps for air in her anxiety.

Ludvík has turned as green as the lawn. Once again he loses his nerve. He isn't even aware of the fact that Anna's fur is still round his neck.

'Maybe they already have all the lowdown about our family. Maybe they know that we only clean the floor at Christmas. And Easter.'

He looks at Anna. There's no doubt that something has crossed his mind. He speaks one word in a whisper.

A whispered word which Anna doesn't follow.

'Dust!' The word comes in a low hiss.

He kneels down once again. Then stands up before going to the dresser and taking from it the upside-down plate with the candle still stuck to it. A box of matches is lying on the sideboard. Full of worry he breaks one match before managing to light another.

With the lighted candle he returns to the sink. Kneels again till he brings the candle right up to Ear.

Everywhere around there's a downy layer of dust. Ludvík draws a line in the dust with his finger.

So that Anna can see. He shows her the finger.

And then with a second finger he very carefully touches Ear. Gently trails a finger over Ear. Lifts the finger up. Not a trace of dust! Shows it to Anna, who is already kneeling next to Ludvík in order to hold the candle for him. He needs both hands free.

With one hand he gingerly lifts Ear a few centimetres into the air, making sure he doesn't pull the wires out of their buttonhole sockets.

Enabling him to feel under Ear with his finger.

Beneath the prism there's the same layer of dust that was all around it.

Cagily he returns the thing to its position.

With bated breath he stands up.

Anna stands up too.

Ludvík blows out the candle. Takes Anna by the hand.

Leads her away from the hall.

But they don't go upstairs. They go to a door leading somewhere they haven't been to. Directly under the staircase.

They are in the other loo. The one that's blocked.

The toilet bowl is flooded with water right up to the top.

'What were we saying in the kitchen?' asks Ludvík. In a half-strangled voice. He's suffocating in his pyjamas.

'In the kitchen... what were we actually talking about?'

'All sorts of things. It's the place where we talk about everything. Do you think it's been there a long time?' asks Anna.

'It's not been there long,' says Ludvík. 'It doesn't look as if it's been there long.'

'The last time we 'slept' in the kitchen was a week ago. Do you think it was already there then?'

Ludvík looks at Anna. He would like to say something harsh to her. That he wished he only had her worries.

'The stink in here is driving me mad,' he says. 'Can't you at least open the window?'

He looks at the window.

'I can't reach it,' says Anna.

Ludvík stretches as far as he can. Reaches for the sky. Manages as far as the window. Fumbles for the handle. And feels something on the window ledge. Gropes at it.

Slides his fingers over it.

It feels like a small prism.

'Bring me a chair,' he hisses.

'Bring a chair here. Move it!'

Once he has a four-legged stool and a chair on top of it, he can be the acrobat and climb. While Anna keeps hold of the wobbly pyramid, he sees on the narrow window ledge the same bug that had been lying in the kitchen at the foot of the sink!

A black prism with buttonholes.

Another case of two wires anchored in socket holes covered in layers of paint.

Ludvík doesn't touch the object. He spends a few seconds staring at Ear Two.

He gets his breath back and then climbs down, almost falling from the stool.

He pushes Anna out of the loo. Shuts the door.

Leaves the chair and the stool where they are.

'There's another one in there,' he whispers.

He starts running up the stairs.

The expression on his face would suit an advanced state of madness.

He goes straight to the loo.

Anna follows at Ludvík's heels.

Without a moment's delay he is standing on the toilet bowl so that he can see the window.

The window here is much lower down. There's nothing on the ledge. He gives a sigh of relief. This little detail seems like a drop of luck in a sea of misfortune. He shuts the door behind Anna.

'There isn't one here,' he says.

He's thinking hard. Trying to sort out the ideas in his mind.

'Tondl's wife told me something,' Anna whispers. 'She said that when they want to listen in, they have to park some sort of green car close to the house. It looks like those the post office uses. Like a tiny bus. No windows in it. With a special antenna on the roof. She painted what one looked like for me. It looks like... like a...'

Anna happens to be looking up at that moment. She goes silent. Her mouth is open to finish the sentence with a word. But the word will not come.

She just raises a hand. Points out to Ludvík a line of pipes leading from the cistern to the wall. There's space between the white pipes and the wall.

About enough to fit three thumbs.

Or in this case a white prism!

With the same buttonholes.

Exactly the same. Except for the colour.

Ludvík can already see Ear Three.

He sees that even the wires here are white.

Anna and Ludvík back away from the loo.

He recognises that there will even be one in the bathroom.

It is here that he spends the most time tracking down Ear Four.

Both of them hunt for it.

Anna is kneeling on the ground.

Ludvík stands on the bath while drops of sweat cover his temple and forehead.

They let the water run from all the taps. To take the edge off Ear's sharp hearing.

And then, while he's perched on the edge of the bath and looking behind the boiler tank, he happens to glance at the ground. Behind the bath. Anna's undies lie there in a heap where he's chucked them. He steps down from the bath. Lifts up a tangle of knickers, slips and bras.

Just the place for a prism.

The foot of the bath.

Finding his hands full of underthings, Ludvík hangs it this time from the door handle himself.

They are both standing in the corridor.

'Ludo!'

'Shhh!'

'Where can we speak?'

'Nowhere!' he says. 'There's nowhere left!'

'You know where? Upstairs,' Anna whispers to him. 'On the balcony.'

They head for the stairs, which continue up from the first floor. To the attic and balcony. On the staircase there's a wooden gate that reaches right up to the ceiling. Ludvk pulls the handle. But the gate is locked.

Anna reaches under the carpet. Pulls out a key.

Swiftly unlocks the gate.

'Why do you always lock the lad up in here?' he asks, regardless of everything. 'If something happened, he wouldn't be able to get out of the house.'

'So that he won't go gadding about the place. When we're not here.'

Ludvík stops suddenly.

'It wasn't Ludi gadding about the place?' he asks.

61

He sees it all clearly now.

How he'd been looking for the key in the kitchen.

And how it was finally found in the door to the hall!

On the inside of the door!

And how by pressing the handle the unlocked door opened easily.

And just as clearly, he sees the moment when his torch happened to light upon the open door in the cellar.

Leading to the garden!

The garden is already full of screeching birds.

The night sky has hardly gone away. Objects are still tinted blue. The wind has dropped.

It's cold on the balcony, but it's a cold neither Anna nor Ludvík feels.

'I would have seen it,' says Anna. Her teeth are chattering. 'If it had been there a long time. I would have seen it just as I saw it a moment ago.'

'They put it there today,' says Ludvík. There's a clothesline either side of his head. Anna has had them installed there permanently. He leans his back against the rough surface of the wall. It's a relatively small balcony. Jutting out from the roof and half covered by an overhang.

'They were here earlier, before we arrived!' he says. 'We came back too soon. You remember that police agent? The one next to the car? When we were leaving? That's what he was saying. Only it didn't dawn on me at the time.'

The young officer saying to Ludvík: 'You're leaving already?'
In a matter-of-fact way. Just before their car pulled up.

The officer looking at his watch.

And at Ludvík.

'Didn't you like it with us?' were the words he used.

Ludvík seeing that Jindřich wasn't there. Just a chauffeur
he didn't know in his place.

Saying: 'That's not my car.'

And so on.

Finally the Comrade arrives. Still in a coat.

The event manager leads him in.

'Now who's going to be in the picture with me? Which of these lasses want to be snapped in my company? They won't tell on me, will they? They don't want me going home to a cold stove.' The ones within earshot give themselves over to a bout of chuckling. But the platform is deserted. Just the chairs have decided to stay. And the armchair in the middle. Only the soldiers are already in position. With the banner.

'Comrades, Comradesses...' The event manager is so afraid he may have an event to manage in his pants.

'Honourable comrades! Distinguished comradesses...!'

He calls out in desperation. His voice falters. He claps his hands.

'Lights! Why aren't the lights on?'

The spotlights come on.

'Outstandingly productive comrades! Outstandingly productive comradesses!'

The Comrade narrows his eyes against the glare of the lights and spots Ludvík.

With Cejnar. He stops to reflect for a while. Trying to place Ludvík. Ludvík manages a fatuous smile. It's all he can do to stop himself from giving the Comrade a prompt.

'Hail to labour' he comes out with in a servile manner.

'Ah....!' says the Comrade As if he has just remembered. But at once the self-satisfied look drains from his face.

'Did I want to ask you something?' He addresses the question to himself. Takes time to think about it. Looks at Ludvík the way we normally look at a tombstone.

Someone trained in servility helps him off with his coat.

'If you would be so kind as to arrange your hair a little!' mumbles the photographer. 'Just a little, just a wee bit...'

'Yes, yes, all right.'

'Comrade, you might wish to spend a moment... before I summon the ranks with a drum roll!' says the event manager. 'Powder your nose! Tidy yourself up a bit.'

'Why would that be...?' asks the Comrade 'Am I an actress in the music hall?' He takes out his comb. Applies it to his head. 'I have a comb, hands too. I think I might ask this comradess to lend me her pocket mirror...!'

The woman in question at once pulls a pocket mirror out of a small bag. Holds it out so that the Comrade can see himself in it. Embarrassment means a shaking hand. And she holds the mirror back to front before correcting herself.

'There's a few hairs on the old dog yet... so why would you be sending me off to clean up? Are you worried that my looks might make the camera lens explode?'

Loud guffaws.

Once again the Comrade's tired eyes land on Ludvík. He takes no pleasure in looking at his face. It's as if he's succumbing to a wave of nausea.

'I think I had something to ask you here,' he says. 'At least, that's the feeling I have. Have we spoken?'

'No,' says Ludvík.

'No?' repeats the Comrade 'No?' He sighs. 'Anyway, it's too late to change things anymore,' he adds. 'Nothing you can do and nothing I can do.'

Ludvík thinks that the Comrade's outstretched hand is meant for him. His own hand shoots out from his side. Expecting it to be clasped. But the Comrade is holding his hand out to the president of the national assembly who's standing next to Ludvík.

There's a moment of embarrassment before Ludvík awkwardly lowers his arm. The Comrade is already leaving. He doesn't pay attention to Ludvík at all. He is talking some matter over with the president of the national assembly.

Those being honoured fall into line once again.

Ludvík stands aside.

'Hang on a minute,' he says in a startled voice, speaking to Cejnar. He's just seen Stanislav.

Stanislav is carrying two full glasses and looking around. He's searching for Ludvík.

Ludvík retreats behind a larger group of guests and looks at his watch.

'Is that the time? I'll be damned!' He bids a hurried farewell to Cejnar. 'You haven't seen Anna, have you?'

'Rushing away already? Where are you scurrying off to? Aren't we going to slip off to the back for our own little night office?'

He is pulling some cards out of his pocket surreptitiously. Showing them to Ludvík.

But Ludvík has already turned his back on him.

'I didn't invite them. I didn't give him the keys!' he says to Anna. Sounding dejected. He's not the same person anymore. Suddenly neither of them is what they were.

'They didn't come for the booze,' says Ludvík. 'They came to finish off their work.'

It's getting lighter all the time.

They are still on the balcony.

Without looking, Ludvík turns over the laundry basket in order to sit on it. A simple operation but he can't manage it properly in his state of agitation. The basket is crumpling under his weight.

'They'd taken away the suitcase already. It was in the cellar. I can remember that it was in the cellar.'

'Why ever can't you write what you want to? Or read the books you want to read?'

'You can do anything. Until they need to have something against you.'

Anna has her arms full of blankets. She hands one to Ludvík. And slippers. The worn-out pair. From the bathroom.

She wraps a blanket round herself. And stands still. Beside Ludvík. And then lights two cigarettes.

Giving one to him.

'When they came!' Ludvík is running over the details. 'I went out of the kitchen. Taking Stanislav to the loo. You weren't in the kitchen either.'

'Yes,' Anna remembers. 'He was in the toilet. Also in the bathroom. He could have done it there. But in the bathroom he wasn't alone. You were there with him...!'

Stanislav saying: 'I think I've left my coat in there.'

Ludvík leaving the bathroom.

Stanislav's coat lying in the loo. Its sleeves inside out.

Ludvík trying to put them right. Slipping his jacket off and then slipping his sweater off. Feeling hot.

Putting his jacket back on.

And returning to the bathroom.

'It doesn't matter now,' he says to Anna. 'It doesn't matter anymore.'

'But Stanislav is your friend from army days!'

'When we were in the army together! That was a century ago. Friend in lore, friend no more.'

'Why? But why? Tell me why! Why all this?'

'They knew I'd get wind of Košara there. They wanted to know what we'd say about it at home. So that they'd have something against him. And against me... they know that we only do our talking in the kitchen, the bathroom and the loo. So they made sure they were bugged too.'

Ludvík stubs out his cigarette against the wall. He throws the butt over the railing of the balcony. He flicks away the butt with two fingers. A habit practised to such perfection that he probably isn't aware of it now.

'No one can... there's nowhere else to talk! They know that! Everyone knows that', Ludvík goes on. 'Not even the Comrade can talk wherever he likes.'

'But the Comrade doesn't have anyone looking down on him,' says Anna. 'Who could bug the Comrade?'

Ludvík lifts the jaundiced eyes of a careworn and sunken face to look at Anna. His features have been put on the rack by a sleepless night. He has a stoop. It's as if he's struggling against some great inner burden.

'How come? What do you mean?' he says. 'Everyone has someone lording it over them.'

'But they've simply planted the bugs in plain sight. We'd have seen them in the morning, wouldn't we?'

'In the morning! That's enough for them and with time to spare! Don't forget how many times they can be here before morning! As many times as they want! A snap of the fingers and here they are again. Now they can't listen to us any more... that means they'll be here like greased lightning! Hang on a moment... there's something coming!'

They both hear the sound of a car approaching the villa. The tarmac is not on the balcony side of the house. The car drives by their house without stopping. The sound fades into the distance.

'Don't you have another bottle somewhere?' asks Ludvík. He's looking at Anna.

'Little Annie of the nursery rhyme?' he says. 'With her green bottles hanging on the wall somewhere... am I right? That's the fifth of my sentences,' he admits in a moment of self-deprecation.

He tries to smile. As he does so his face manages to look nearly human for a moment. It's almost moving. He looks like a helpless, cornered ash-grey mouse.

He gets up. Chucks away the blanket. Onto the basket. But then he picks it up again. And puts it round Anna's shoulders.

'I've also got a bottle ready to fall!' he says.

As if something has just crossed his mind.

Anna doesn't notice anything. Not even the fleeting touch of his hand on her shoulder.

'Wait here!' he says. 'Hang on a while!'

She sits down on the empty basket. In a cold shiver.

In the garden steam is rising from the ground.

She leans forward with her face in her hands and her elbows on her knees. Rubs her nose with her fingertips. And her eyebrows. Now that Ludvík's not there she's on the verge of tears. Her whole face is trembling. She snuffles as if she's going down with a cold. And then goes into a tearful, explosive coughing fit.

She gets up.

Clears her throat. Spits over the balcony into the garden. And stands rooted to the spot. It's getting light.

Anna spots a closed-up, windowless little bus. She can only see part of it because it's hidden behind a transformer. It could indeed be taken for a post van.

Were it not for the antenna on the roof with its many arms.

Looking like a photographer's tripod without the camera attached.

It's in the narrow lane between the villas.

On the opposite side to the tarmac road. There's a spot for playing volleyball there with a taut net.

'Ludo!' Anna turns towards the door.

She calls inside the house: 'Ludo!'

She tosses the blankets aside.

'Ludvík!' she calls out.

'Ludo!' she calls out along the corridor.

'Ludo!' she calls, lowering her voice inside the house.

She doesn't want to wake the boy.

She runs down the stairs.

'Ludo!'

Calling out to the floor below. Straining to see from the bend in the staircase into the empty hall, just to make sure.

'Ludo...?'

Now she starts running towards his study.

Seizes hold of the door handle.

But the door is unrelenting.

'Ludo!'

Tries the handle once more.

'Are you in there?'

Anna moves to the bedroom. Heads for the connecting door with his study.

Finds it locked like the other one.

Works on the handle here too.

'Ludo!' she calls out. More loudly now.

Seeing that this door is also locked.

And can only be locked from the inside.

And that can only be for one reason.

Which sends a shiver through her whole being.

Anna wrenches at the handle. Bangs on the door with her palms.

'Ludo! Open up!' she cries out. Yelling now.

She doesn't realise that she's yelling.

She goes back once again to the door in the corridor.

As if there might be something different about it this time.

Unaware that she's just wasting time.

Wrenches at the handle, beats on the door, throws the whole weight of her body against it, trying to force it open.

Tearfully she cries:

'Ludi! Don't do it! Ludi!'

Back to the bedroom.

Beating on the door with both fists.

'If you do that,' she cries out at the top of her voice, 'I'm going to do it too!'

Then she dashes across to the window.

She trips over objects in the bedroom and knocks something over but doesn't notice. Her mind is only on the bedroom window which is on the same level as the study window. Frantically she opens it, banging the frame in the process. It's a wonder that she doesn't shatter the glass.

She's already climbing through the window.

Now she's kneeling on it, with quite a large drop to the garden beneath her. There's a ledge beneath the window that is broad enough. Maybe thirty centimetres. Encircling the house like the ring around Saturn.

Anna is kneeling on that ledge now.

It's a risky procedure.

She stays on her knees, using them to inch her way along the ledge, her pyjama top slipping halfway down her back. Breathing heavily, Anna gropes forward with her hands, overcoming an awkward narrowing of the ledge. She stretches out a hand, reaching right across to the study window. And now, in a voice low but audible, because all is quiet and she's directly in front of the window frame, she calls to Ludvík:

'Ludi! Ludo!'

She tries to act quickly, without losing so much as a second. The look on her face shows that she has just one thought in her head. She is afraid that perhaps it is already too late, and that before she makes it to his window the shot will ring out.

She uses the flat of her hand to smash the glass pane.

Splinters of glass spurt out like tears, falling downwards beside the wall of the villa. Their flight seems unreal to Anna, the veil of moisture over her eyes clouding her sight. Then all those tears are shattered once more on the cement path below.

With the opening in the window still a narrow one, she pulls out more pieces of glass so she can reach through her arm and get to the handle. Because the window opens inwards and is a double one, she has to smash even the inner window with her fist. She does so.

'Ludo!' she calls out. 'Don't do it! Don't do it, I'm begging you!'

Her arm is already covered in blood from the scratches and pricks inflicted by fragments of glass.

Then she bursts into the room.

Best to say she tumbles into the study rather than enters it.

She looks around for him, with eyes for nothing apart from Ludvík.

'Ludi!'

70

He is sitting at the desk.

Looking uncomfortable, leaning backwards.

Anna gives a cry.

Because it looks as if he's already done it and she didn't hear the shot or thought it was something else.

And she is deceived by the poor light.

Ludvík has turned the lights off, leaving the study in nothing more than the thin light of daybreak.

The most disconcerting impression of all is Ludvík motionless. There isn't the slightest movement, not the merest hint of motion or of turning round, even in the face of breaking glass, Anna's constant yelling and later her tumble onto the floor. She collapses onto a plant stand right under the window, picks herself up from fragments of pot, spilt earth and splinters of glass, and in one bound is at his side, seizing his head in both hands and sensing that it's a live one, running her hands over his face, neck, forehead, shoulders as if she's blind, in order to make sure that he is still alive.

'What...were you thinking of doing?' she mutters. Her mouth is full of saliva and words which she can't even hear herself, a keening tone to her voice as she grows calm in the realisation that the worst has not yet happened, and yet grows anxious in the knowledge of what things could have come to.

'You wouldn't really do it...? You wouldn't really do it to us...?'

At first glance Anna can't miss the open revolver case lying on the desk in front of Ludvík, but she doesn't see the pistol anywhere, even though the first thing she does is look along one arm hanging down and then the other, on the table in a slightly bent position, beside an empty piece of paper and a pencil, as if he had prepared himself to write something and had then given up on the idea.

She cannot see the pistol anywhere.

'Give me... the revolver!' she whispers to him.

Still not herself.

Not in the least aware of the bloody marks on her body, she kisses Ludvík, though not in an amorous way but like the maternal smothering that mothers sometimes give when danger has passed and they cover their children's entire faces with kisses.

'Where've you put the revolver? You've got to give it to me. You can't do this to us! I won't allow it...!'

Until this moment he hasn't moved and hasn't spoken a word.

Even now he doesn't look at Anna.

'They took the pistol away,' he says.

The eyes he raises to Anna are of someone who is no longer a person.

All self-assurance has drained out of his face.

'When they want it done, they'll do it themselves,' he says.

He is devoid of all emotion now. And self-pity. He is just noting a fact.

71

'I will never let you go,' says Anna. 'I will stay with you. Let them arrest me with you!'

Anna is kneeling beside the seated Ludvík. Her arms enfolding his neck. Hugging his head and body to herself, brushing his face against hers, rubbing her face up and down against his, in a rhythm of love resigned to fate.

They have been pushed so far that they aren't even aware of what's happening.

'What are we...?' she begins to say. In a low voice. With dry lips that feel as if they've been glued together. 'Have we become slaves...? Are we even human?'

She raises her head. To the ceiling. To the four walls. To Ear.

'What do you want from us? What do you want... Ear? Do you want us to kill ourselves? Is that what you want? Or do you want to kill us yourself?'

Anna gets up. And listens.

As if she could get an answer if she waited long enough. Then she goes to the door. Unlocks it. Keeps the key wrapped in her hand.

She also unlocks the door to the bedroom. Takes this key out of the lock too.

Goes out of the bedroom into the corridor. Heads for the loo.

Throws both keys into the bowl. And flushes.

Looks at the device. Wedged behind the pipe.

And makes a decision.

Climbs onto the toilet. Raises her right arm. And whispers:

'Not even you are allowed to listen in the lavatory, Ear!' She takes hold of the apparatus and holds it away from her body as if it's something alive.

Thin wires hang from the prismatic device trailing their way to jack plugs.

Anna hurries out to the bathroom. Her stomach leans into the bath as she reaches behind it. Her face is right above the second bug.

'You're not even allowed to listen in the bathroom…!'

She now has one listening device in each hand. Quietly passes the study. On tiptoes. Making sure Ludvík doesn't hear her.

Dashes downstairs. To the kitchen. Kneels down on the lino so that she can crawl under the sink.

'You're not even allowed to listen in the kitchen! You must know that. Do you hear me? Catch what I'm saying?'

'The kitchen, the bathroom, the loo… this is where even state officials can have words… or sex, when they can… or visitors…! Get that into your lug, Ear!'

She rips out the third device.

Then she gets up. Passes through the hall. To the flooded loo. And flings all the devices into the pool of filth.

Then she raises her head to the small window-ledge above.

Where the fourth device is always listening.

'I've thrown your ears down the pan!' she says. 'It might make you finally send a plumber here. It's the downstairs loo. In the hall. Comrade Kosař has made a note of it three times already…'

Now she climbs onto the toilet seat and scales the pipes above. Much more skilfully than Ludvík earlier on.

She rips off the fourth device and drops it into the bowl from high up.

'Greetings to the Comrade!' she says.

Ludvík and Anna are getting dressed in the bathroom.

Ludvík is back in his jersey. With a lounge jacket.

Anna has a jacket and skirt set.

Ready for a journey.

She packs a snack in his briefcase. In a bag. Apples.

'Don't be silly!' Ludvík says. 'They won't let us keep that. They won't leave us with anything. Do you think it's like... a trip to Karlštejn?'

'Maybe they'll let us.'

So much has been crammed into the briefcase that she can hardly close it.

'The main thing is that they put Ludi with Aunt Božena.'

'What else would they do with him?' asks Ludvík. 'They can't be bothered with the brat.'

Ludvík picks up the things Anna has prepared for him from the chair. There are several bank deposit books. He thumbs through them. And a handful of gold ornaments of all types.

Rings. Bracelets. Lockets hanging from chains as necklaces.

'The letter for Auntie,' he whispers. 'Where have you put the letter?'

Anna passes over to him a sealed letter.

They both leave the bathroom in silence.

They move around the house as if it's no longer theirs.

Warily. On tiptoe.

They don't speak.

Ludvík is the first to the window

Anna breathing heavily at his side.

Both watch the garden coming into the light of day. And the gate.

So far the street is deserted.

Ludvík checks his watch. Four o'clock.

'It's the hour they come!' he says. 'Between four and five!'

He's whispering to Anna, his lips almost inside her ear. On account of Ear.

'It's already light, but everyone's still asleep,' he explains.

He sounds almost matter of fact about it. As if it was something that didn't really concern the two of them.

He turns round.

Anna follows behind Ludvík. Both head up the stairs two steps at a time...

They are careful when they enter the boy's room. Anna opens the door very gently and then quietly shuts it in the same way.

The lad is sleeping in a small room with a sloping ceiling. The way attic rooms tend to be. He's kicked off the bedclothes in his sleep.

Anna puts the covers back over him. Gently.

He's a typical boy, tousled and freckled. About ten. Nothing special about him. Clearly takes after Ludvík. Lying on his back with his mouth open, hands raised to nestle by his face while he sleeps. Palms facing up.

Anna sits at the bedside while Ludvík takes a look around. Spots his satchel by the desk. Goes to it. Kneels on the ground. Tries to open it. Tackles the nickel-plated clasps trying not to make a noise. Makes some anyway. Gets the satchel open.

Puts the bank deposit books among the lad's school-books and exercise books. The jewels he slips into a laminated pencil case. Then he adds a letter addressed to:

AUNTIE

He shuts the satchel again. Puts it back where he found it.

'Come on!' he says to Anna, who is on the verge of tears.

'Come on! Let him sleep! Let him sleep while he can.'

'What did they say... about him at school?'

The two of them are back on the balcony. They have taken a couple of chairs there. On a box of some kind they have their makeshift 'table' with mugs of coffee, the cake leftovers and a bottle of cognac.

They both have blankets around their shoulders.

'He was with those boys who spat at the portrait,' says Anna.

Ludvík pauses as he stirs his coffee.

'Our Ludi?'

'No one said he was there,' explains Anna. 'But when there was an inquiry into it, he went to the head teacher and said he was one of those spitting.'

Ludvík stays quiet. His face gives nothing away.

Anna gets up. Looks into the garden.

She sees the long ladder lying between the trees.

'See that!' she says. 'Take a look! They left the ladder lying there!'

She shows him with her hand.

'Where do you think they were trying to climb...?'

Ludvík pours some cognac.

'Have we had a toast? Have we drunk to our anniversary yet?'

'The anniversary was yesterday. It's already the eighteenth,' says Anna.

They clink glasses. And drink the toast.

Anna leans back to look at a swallow's nest in the corner of the little half-roof above her head. The small opening in the nest is the wrong way round, pointing downwards. Towards them. A swallow's nest rearranged to be without any swallows.

'Look up there!' she says. 'A swallow's nest! Do you know I've never noticed it before? Have you ever noticed that nest yourself...?'

He doesn't even look. He wouldn't have seen anything suspicious about it anyway because it is so high up.

He would have needed to look in more detail. And above all from close up. But there is no time any more for all that.

Because at that very moment the bell rings.

'Did you hear a car?'

'No.'

Both Ludvík and Anna are on their feet now.

Still on the balcony.

'Nothing came by.'

'It's not the gate!' says Ludvík. He takes in the regularity of the ringing.

'That's the 'phone.'

The 'phone rings on, regular and relentless.

Ludvík heads downstairs about two steps ahead of Anna.

Looks at his watch. Five o'clock exactly.

'Five in the morning,' he says.

They are both standing above the device.

Ludvík reaches for the receiver. He's trembling. Almost drops it.

'Hallo?' he says.

The other end of the line is unintelligible to Anna. She can only make out the droning voice.

But Ludvík evidently understands.

'Hail to labour,' he says. To whomever. Sounding respectful.

Anna wants to get close to the receiver in order to listen in.

Ludvík motions her to stay standing and stay quiet.

'Yes...' he is saying. 'Indeed...'

And then once more. 'Indeed... indeed...'

He loosens his collar.

'Certainly... of... of course... yes, indeed.'

Silence at the other end. You could hear that they've rung off.

'Hail to labour,' says Ludvík once again. Though the line has gone dead by now.

He continues holding the receiver to his ear looking half-demented.

Then holds it slightly further from his ear. Then his arm drops, still holding on to the receiver.

Finally he returns it to the cradle in slow motion.

And sits on the stairs.

'That was the Comrade,' he says.

Without waiting for Anna to ask first.

'Now? In the middle of the night?'

Anna is looking at Ludvík.

'Dressing-down, was it?' She speaks in a whisper. Wants to escape the attention of Ear.

'He gave you a rocket?'

Ludvík puts his head in his hands.

As if it is sore from its own weight.

'He made me minister,' he says.

His voice sounds flat.

'To replace Košara,' he says.

78

He stays sitting there for a long time.

Anna doesn't ask him anything. She goes first to switch off the lights.

She turns them off everywhere. In the kitchen. On the stairs down to the cellar.

In the cellar. In the laundry room.

She goes back to Ludvík.

There is now a milky pallor in the hall.

From the window the pale light of dawn spreads to the staircase.

Anna sits down beside Ludvík on the stairs.

'Don't accept it!' she says. 'Ludo... don't take it.'

'He didn't ask me whether I wanted it or not. He was informing me of my appointment.'

She takes his hands. Wraps his hands in hers. Whispers to him.

'We'll go away, Ludo! You can still be director. Like Cejnar! What does he have to worry about? Nothing!'

She strokes his hands while looking ill at ease. Blinks her eyes. Pulls out a handkerchief. Blows her nose.

It's the beginnings of a cold.

'They can't make you a minister now! How can they when they were here... when they heard everything? Ear knows by now that you're the one who wrote the report... how can they make you a minister now?'

'That's just the point,' he says 'Now they can do it.'

He stands up.

Anna gets up too.

They leave the telephone on the stairs.

They both need to step over the cord as they make their way down. To the hall. Then to the kitchen.

Anna puts herself in front of Ludvík.

He has to stop.

Wearily unbuttons his jacket and sweater.

'I'm afraid,' whispers Anna.

She clasps hold of Ludvík. Her words are almost inaudible.

'Ludo... I'm scared...!'

It's clear that the whole thing fills her with fear.

'We are all scared,' he replies.

The car horn wakes Anna up.

It immediately sets off a bout of sneezing. Her nose is red and runny from her cold.

Anna and Ludvík had been sleeping in the kitchen. On a carpet covered with a bedsheet. Each of them underneath something like a dog's blanket.

Beneath the blankets they are both naked.

Anna has the fox fur round her neck. She hasn't taken it off.

On the lino at the top of the makeshift bed there's an empty bottle of cognac and glasses. On a plate lies a long and almost untouched Hungarian salami. And a knife.

And around the salami a few peelings.

And then there's the ashtray. The packet of cigarettes. The lighter.

'Ludo!' Anna is shaking her husband awake. 'Ludo! Your car's here. Jindřich is here already!'

Ludvík is already dressed. Wearing a suit we've never seen him in before. A very nice one.

Anna straightens his tie for him.

Anna is wearing her crumpled flannel pyjamas.

At the last minute, Ludvík lugs the shaggy carpet from the kitchen to the hall.

And folds the bedsheet clumsily before stuffing it back in its home behind the cushions of the armchair.

'I'll deal with that!' says Anna. 'As if I wouldn't tidy things up...'

Her looks are puffy in the morning light. Unappealing.

'I know you will!' he says.

She goes with him to the gate in pyjamas. Unshod.

'For God's sake, don't shuffle around barefoot... when you've got a cold! You'll be blowing your nose for a month!'

Ludvík pauses at the gate before opening it.

'If I hadn't taken the job...' he says. The remark comes out of the blue.

'Someone worse would have taken it. After all I was a friend of Košara.'

'I won't be moving to Košara's villa though,' says Anna. 'I can make that a condition, can't I? They'll come up with... something else. I wouldn't be able to sleep over there!'

'Very well!' he says. 'I'll insist on it! As a matter of principle.'

Then Ludvík came to be ferried across Prague.

The city was bathed in sunlight. Beautiful as always and at the same time indifferent. Its buildings and churches were ancient enough to have long memories.

The pigeons flew up from the tower of St Nicholas. The bells were ringing. And Ludvík foists his packet of cigarettes on Jindřich.

'Have a smoke!' he says.

Jindřich takes one. Ludvík has a cigarette too.

Jindřich uses the car lighter first for Ludvík and then for himself. It comes as part of the car's fittings.

Ludvík is sitting in the front seat. His left arm is stretched out over the backrest behind Jindřich. He drums his fingers on it. Less in agitation than in a show of bonhomie.

He has adjusted his position. His back is turned towards the door so that he partly faces Jindřich. A stance to make his importance immediately apparent.

They brake sharply. A girl was crossing the street. Not looking where she was going. It turns out to be all right.

'Watch out, lass,' says Ludvík. 'That would have been a waste!' They both laugh from inside the car.

The limousine stops in front of the ministry.

Ludvík gets out.

There is already someone waiting for him on the steps. One is the chap who was speaking with him at the reception. He holds out his hand to Ludvík.

He greets Ludvík with 'Hail to labour, Comrade!' He then adds: 'We've been through everything.' He's rushing his words. 'Been through everything. You can be assured that the whole central committee is on your side one hundred per cent.'

The head of the secretariat is also awaiting his arrival.

He is the sort of obliging fellow who looks like all the other little men who hang around big men brown-nosing.

He resembles the middle-aged sales assistants who sell cosmetics in a specialist drugstore.

'Comrade Minister,' he says with a bow. Waits until Ludvík himself offers to shake hands. And then grasps the minister's hand in grateful appreciation.

As if it is something sacred.

'Comrade Minister, the commission is expecting you.'

They are already in the reception area. Surrounded by burly blue-collar doormen.

Ludvík holds out a hand. To all of them. And says to the fawning flunky in their hearing: 'I'll have to stop to pick up the tools of my trade first, won't I?'

He goes out to the paternoster lift. Overhears the doorman talking about him behind his back.

'He's all right. Decent chap, that one.'

The remarks please him.

He goes into his former office.

On the door there is an inscription: DEPUTY MINISTER.

Konvičková, his secretary, is standing by the table. She mumbles a greeting. She can hardly speak. Her eyes are red. She's fighting back tears. A comely, well-rounded young woman.

With a fur round her neck.

'Hail to labour and all that, Olinka!' says Ludvík. 'We're on the move. Start packing our things.'

Her face lights up. In a flash she is all brightness.

'Really? She almost wails in delight. 'Yes... Comrade Minister.'

She looks at Ludvík as if she's having a divine visitation.

The fawning flunky follows Ludvík into the office.

'Comrade Minister... if I have understood correctly... your intention is to take Comrade Konvičková to your office?'

'Just so,' he says.

The look he gives the head of the secretariat is almost one of surprise.

'Perhaps it might be unwise to break up a team of builders! After all, we are builders, aren't we? Are we?'

At last the brown-noser leads him through the door marked MINISTER!

Though there's another team of secretaries to pass first.

An attractive middle-aged lady gets up from the table. Black hair – a lot of it. Heading halfway down her back.

Wearing a blouse that is glossy and tightly fitting. Everything about her is tight-fitting. She is another one with red eyes. And another one with a fur. Thrown with a certain nonchalance around her low white neckline.

With exquisite taste.

She is another one who greets him rather tearfully. But tries to preserve her dignity. The air of the aristocrat. An echo of her noble forbears as they marched to the scaffold.

'Hail to labour, Comrade Jablonecká,' says Ludvík. He's looking at the silver-blue fur. And at what it's wound around. But now he must move on to the door. The door to his new office.

It's a double door. Between them there's a fairly sizeable space. To make sure that no sounds get through to the minister from outside.

It is in this small area that Ludvík comes to a halt with the fawning flunky. The two of them are almost squashed together.

'Keep Comrade Jablonecká in my secretarial team too,' he says.

'Don't go moving her anywhere! She's got experience and she's been well run-in here... and we're pressed for time now. There's so much to sort out!'

He says this in a by-the-way manner.

'My thinking too,' confirms the flunky.

He knows exactly what Ludvík is saying.

82

Ludvík chairs the ministerial commission.

In the big committee room.

Twenty men are sitting round a large table. Each has a pile of papers in front of him.

Ludvík casts his eyes at the one on top:

REPORT ON THE PREMATURE CLOSURE OF A LOCAL BRICKWORKS.

'Hmmmm!' He swallows. 'The brickworks report,' he begins. Without taking his eyes off the papers. The words stick in his throat. 'It's not on the table... it's... under the table. It's... we're withdrawing the report,' he says.

He turns to the man sitting closest to him. 'Rouchar will put together a committee to start closure proceedings!'

Someone pipes up:

'But... last time we passed a resolution to table the report!'

Ludvík doesn't so much as raise his eyes. He obviously knows who the speaker is.

'Engineer!' he says. 'You will speak when I give you the floor. Do you understand? So that our mouths don't get ahead of our minds. They wouldn't get very far!'

Now he looks up at them all. At every single one.

'I spoke about this yesterday... with the Comrade' he says. 'We must not go against the tide of history. We must not get bogged down over petty details!'

He puts the report to one side. Beside the rest of his pile.

The text facing downwards. The blank back page facing up.

Everyone around the table does the same thing with their reports as Ludvík.

Later he pokes his head into the secretaries' office.

The workmen have just brought in a second table. For Konvičková.

Both the secretaries pipe up at once:

'Is there anything you need, Comrade Minister?'

'No, no,' he says. 'That is... I'll be... right back.'

He goes out into the corridor.

The two secretaries stay standing. Prepared for the possibility of his return. With an assignment to give them.

Ludvík moves down the long corridor.

They are greeting him. He acknowledges them. Steps into the paternoster lift. Goes down to the ground floor. Passes through reception.

'Should I call Jindřich for you, Comrade Minister?'

'No, no!' he tells the doorman.

He goes out into the street. A short way along the pavement. Moving among ordinary people. Crosses to the other side of the street. Looks around. Checks that no one recognises him.

No one knows who he is.

Goes to a 'phone booth. Enters it. Searches his pockets for change. Has to return to the tobacconist. Plucks out a hundred-crown note. To get change. Leaves the tobacconist a fat tip. Then makes his call. Waits a moment for Anna to pick up.

'It's me,' he says. Keeping his voice down. 'Has Ludi already gone to school? We left...things...in his satchel,' he goes on. His eyes roving up and down the street all the time. But still no one's paying any attention to Ludvík.

'He hasn't gone,' he hears Anna say. The line is hardly audible. 'Ludi doesn't have school today. As I told you, the school's on a work assignment. So I'm keeping him at home.'

Ludvík sighs with relief and hangs up. Leaves the telephone booth. Goes back amongst the people.

At that moment Ludi is playing in the garden. In the summerhouse.

He has a little electrical workshop there. Amongst all the odds and ends he's discovered an old military suitcase. He opens it.

On the inside of the lid there's a photograph. It's of Ludvík. As a soldier. A second lieutenant.

With a lean and hungry look that says he wants something.

There are books in the case. And exercise books. And papers.

Ludi opens one of the books. The frontispiece is a photograph. Lenin. In another of the books it's Trotsky.

And in another someone with a name that is too long.

Nothing of interest to the boy. He looks up at the villa from the summerhouse.

No sign of Mum.

He takes the suitcase and hauls it across the flowerbeds towards the gate.

Mum's paper party hat is fixed on his head.

He heads in front of the house. Towards the bin.

And empties everything inside.

And is happy to have got such a beautiful suitcase.

Which should come in really handy one day.

Nothing happens after that.

Just the binmen passing by.

They empty the bins in front of the villa described in our painstaking narrative.

A few pieces of papers flutter around in the process.

One piece is batted away by a binman and becomes stuck to his glove.

In the bin lorry, seated in the front cabin with the other binman and the driver, he tries to read the capital letters of the handwritten message.

'Look at this, chaps!' he says. 'ONLY SOCIALISM CAN GIVE US FREEDOM AND HAPPINESS!'

'Where do we knock off?' asks the driver. 'At the Dirty Drummer?'

'The Dirty Drummer? No way,' says the other binman. 'Knock off at the Broken Bell! That sloven at the Dirty Drummer last rinsed his beer pipes when the pub was built.'

It was during his military service that Jan Procházka first came across the work of Ernest Hemingway and was inspired to start writing. Hemingway remained a strong influence throughout his career. According to his daughter, the writer Lenka Procházková, he always kept a photograph of Hemingway on his bookshelf, and for years the family assumed it was a relative. In 1961, the year Hemingway died, Procházka visited Cuba and saw the simple white farmhouse where he had lived. His daughter remembers that one of his dreams was to find a similar place to live and write.

Jan Procházka was one of the most popular Czech authors of the 1960s and is still read widely, but he is best known for his collaboration as a screenwriter with the filmmaker Karel Kachyňa. Most of his prose writings have a parallel life in film, and *Ear* is no exception. Its 1990 edition, the first to appear in Czechoslovakia, two decades after it was banned, bears the subtitle "film story", and this has been kept in all subsequent editions. The book can be read as a screenplay, but this does not in any way detract from its value as a literary text. In his 1968 collection of articles and essays *Politics for Everyone,* Procházka wrote that, just like a play or a novella, "writing a screenplay is storytelling" and not a "set of technical directions". In *Ear* simple sentences or sometimes just fragments of sentences set each scene and frame the dialogue with an economy that is overtly poetic. Like Hemingway, Procházka distils surface details without explanation or interpretation. The power of the writing often lies in what remains unsaid. Just as Hemingway honed his craft during his years as a journalist, Procházka owed his economy of style at least in part to the discipline of screenwriting.

Procházka is a master of dialogue. The dialogue in *Ear* is realistic, full of everyday slang (which is challenging for a translator), but at the same time it is pared down and fragmentary, hinting at a hinterland that is painful, unresolved and in the case of this story, sinister. Procházka was an exact contemporary of Harold Pinter, another master of the unsaid or half-said, but unlike Pinter he nearly always remains grounded in time and place. We would be hard pressed to find a scene in *Ear* that could not have happened. If the story seems absurd or surreal, this stems from the grotesque realities of its setting in early 1950s Czechoslovakia. Procházka is at home in the tradition of realism, but, as with Hemingway, it is a concentrated realism that goes beyond the moment. "The writer should not write things which instantly, in the moment they are written, are wiped out like chalk words on a blackboard," he wrote in an undated text which his daughter Lenka found in his drawer after his death.

Ear has also been compared to Edward Albee's *Who's Afraid of Virginia Woolf?* Albee was another contemporary, and Lenka Procházková recalls that her father was hugely impressed when they went to see Mike Nichol's 1966 film adaptation with Richard Burton and Elizabeth Taylor. Like Albee's play, *Ear* opens with a drunken middle-aged couple arriving home after a party and the story takes place in the space of one night. The liquor-fuelled sparring between the two protagonists is central to both texts, as is their sense of being trapped in their roles, and in both there is an uneasy relationship between illusion, self-delusion and reality. They also share many moments of dark humour. But *Ear* has a political side that is specific to Procházka and the extraordinary times he was living through. Although the hell in which they are trapped is partly of their own making, the catalyst for the crisis faced by Anna and Ludvík comes directly from the political reality of the world they are living in. Procházka sets the story in the Stalinist Czechoslovakia of the early 1950s, the time of political purges and show-trials, when a night-time knock on the door could have catastrophic, even fatal, consequences. By the time he was writing *Ear*, towards the end of 1968, this was already history, but the atmosphere of fear had returned. In August 1968, the Soviet Union had led the Warsaw Pact occupation of Czechoslovakia, bringing an end to the reforms of the Prague Spring. In banning the book and the film, the censors unwittingly confirmed the relevance of the story to their own time.

It is one of the paradoxes of the period after 1968 that many of those who were most ruthlessly persecuted had previously been active communists themselves. Jan Procházka was no exception.

During the thaw of the 1960s, he had been one of the country's most visible and overtly political writers, an articulate advocate of reform communism. He had charisma and people who heard him speak in public recall that he radiated energy and authority, "like a bulldozer, with a gift for persuading people that he was right," in the words of the playwright Pavel Kohout. When the Party Secretary Alexander Dubček introduced the radical reforms of the Prague Spring in 1968, many in the younger generation saw Procházka as a future Czechoslovak President, a symbol of "socialism with a human face". All this was to end with the invasion.

Procházka was an early convert to socialism. He was born on 4th February 1929 in Ivančice in South Moravia, the south-eastern corner of today's Czech Republic. It is a small town at the heart of a traditionally Catholic agricultural region known for its vineyards and gentle climate, and Procházka's writing often returns to this rural world. At sixteen he witnessed the Red Army's liberation of his hometown from the roof of his family's farmhouse, and like so many of his generation, he joined the Communist Party as soon as he was old enough, "convinced that socialism would mean a new, more just order." This led to tensions with his father, who as a proudly independent farmer at first resisted joining the local farming collective after the communists came to power in 1948. Procházka left home to study at the Agricultural College in Olomouc, about a hundred kilometres north-east of Ivančice. Soon afterwards he was appointed head of the State Youth Farm in nearby Ondrášov.

His first collection of short stories *A Year in the Life* (1956) is a celebration of collectivisation, based on his experiences on the farm. The book was not a success, and he was quick to recognise its flaws. The stories were formulaic and artificial, driven by his political enthusiasm rather than his powers of observation. His novella *Green Horizons*, written three years later, was very different. It has a similar setting but its portrayal of life in the countryside of the Czech borderlands, resettled after the violent expulsion of the country's German minority, is anything but idyllic. The characters are drawn with a subtlety that challenges the crude templates of socialist realism prevalent at the time, and he writes with the authority of someone familiar with the land. It is lyrical but shuns nostalgia or pathos.

Thanks to the success of *Green Horizons*, Procházka was noticed by the writer František Kožík, who saw a filmic quality to his writing, with its strong characterisation and eye for telling detail. On Kožík's recommendation, he was hired in 1960 as a script editor and then screenwriter at the Barrandov film studios in Prague. Soon afterwards he began to work with Karel Kachyňa, who was five years his senior and already a successful filmmaker. Over the next decade they were to make a dozen films together. Many of these started as short stories or novellas, although Procházka's literary imagination is so closely entwined with film that the roots of film and book are often hard to separate. He became a master of what he called the "literary screenplay". Christopher Isherwood's famous words, "I am a camera with its shutter open," can be applied almost literally to Procházka's writing, but when Isherwood's narrator in *Goodbye to Berlin* adds that he is "quite passive, recording, not thinking," this could hardly be further from Procházka's approach to writing and screenwriting. Procházka is anything but passive, carefully composing every image and every movement, with a clear idea of what he wants to say.

In a rather old-fashioned sense he is a moralist, and this can be seen in all his work during the 1960s. "Don't let anyone tell you otherwise. To espouse the idea of right and wrong is neither stupid, nor is it conformist or conservative," he writes in *Politics for Everyone*. When he talks about his faith in socialism, his interpretation of the word is so broad that it could be replaced with "democracy" or "humanism" without a significant shift in meaning. His moral and political compass is steered by the idea that it is important to watch closely and to see things as they are, to acknowledge society's flaws and where necessary to draw attention to them, but without passing judgment. *Politics for Everyone* begins with the words: "Since time immemorial, the only way we have managed to find truth is by forcing ourselves to overcome our natural inclination to lie."

This moral impulse brings with it an acknowledgement of human frailty. Procházka's protagonists are always flawed, and this is what defines their humanity and makes them attractive. In the story *Magdaléna* from 1963, the heroes are an alcoholic and a prostitute, played brilliantly by Rudolf Hrušinský and Hana Hegerová in Kachyňa's film from the same year. Neither the story nor the film impressed the political establishment – these were hardly role models for a socialist society – but Procházka's defence was simple: this is a story of human hope (*Hope* is also the title of Kachyňa's film), and this is what the two protagonists find in one another. In *Ear*, we are given a similarly nuanced portrait of an imperfect relationship. Anna and Ludvík's marriage is deeply dysfunctional, and their endless sparring occasionally spills over into violence, but for all this rawness, inseparable from the agonisingly claustrophobic situation in which they find themselves, the writer portrays them with sympathy. He pokes fun at his protagonists, but there are moments of tenderness and unexpected poetry.

Often it is the female characters who are developed most strongly in Procházka's work. The short story *Magdaléna* was the fourth in a series of portraits of women, each of which he adapted as a screenplay. Starting with the twelve-year-old Jitka and her unlikely friendship with a hospital patient who is struggling to walk and ending with the eponymous prostitute, each story reminds us in its own way of the gulf between the loudly trumpeted claim that women have achieved equality in socialist society and the reality of their lives. In *Politics for Everyone*, he mocks the poet who claims that "women are flowers and mothers."

Procházka himself was for many years the only man in a household of women, made up of his wife Mahulena, their three daughters, Lenka, Iva and Krista and Mahulena's mother Marie, whose husband had been killed by the Germans during the war. He was devoted to his family and went out of his way to encourage his daughters to think independently. Many of his stories and screenplays have children – girls or boys – as their central figure, rebellious, getting into trouble, but usually with more wisdom than all the adults put together. His daughter Lenka remembers how he would tell her a bedtime story and then hurry to his study to write it up on his typewriter. Lenka and Iva both went on to become successful writers.

Procházka had a gift for putting a deeply human story into the context of broad historical events and in so doing, casting doubt on the prevailing narrative of those events. This is the case with the three best-known films he made with Karel Kachyňa, *Ear* (1970), *Long Live the Republic* (1965) and *Coach to Vienna* (1966). While *Ear* blurs the line between victim and perpetrator at the time of the 1950s purges, the other two films offer an ambivalent view of the liberation of Czechoslovakia at the end of the Second World War. The strongly autobiographical *Long Live the Republic*, set in the rural world of South Moravia at the very end of the war, is not a celebration of victory. The cruelty of war seeps into the peace and is presented in stark contrast with the innocence of a twelve-year-old child, Olin. In *Coach to Vienna*, a young woman, who has seen her husband hanged by the Germans, recognises the humanity of a young German soldier and is unable to kill him in revenge. Criticised for portraying perpetrators as victims, Procházka replied that "most victims of war are innocent. How could it be otherwise? Has it ever been the case that those who are sent to fight have wanted to go to war?"

At the height of his success at the Barrandov studios, Procházka established an unlikely personal friendship – or near-friendship – with the then Czechoslovak President Antonín Novotný. According to Lenka Procházková, it started with a mistake. Novotný had heard a radio report by someone with the same surname talking about agricultural reforms and expressed a desire to meet this young comrade. The wrong Procházka was summoned, but he made such an impression that they began to meet regularly and he became the president's advisor for film. He sat on various official bodies, including the Communist Party's "ideological committee" where he was able to use his influence to help fellow filmmakers, including Jan Němec and Věra Chytilová, to get past the censors. He must have had plenty of glimpses into the murky corridors of power, and these experiences would have helped him when writing the grotesquely realistic scenes at the boozy government reception in *Ear*.

Procházka knew he was treading a fine line. His outspokenness was already being noticed by hardliners and the secret police.

At the Congress of the Union of Czechoslovak Writers in June 1967 he was one of several writers who openly criticised the political status quo. His status as "Candidate for the Central Committee of the Communist Party" was suspended, and there could have been more serious consequences, had it not been for the reforms of the Prague Spring that began a few months later. Procházka became a voice for change. At a public discussion in March 1968, he gave a now legendary speech, in which he argued that elections in communist Czechoslovakia were nothing more than a façade, "an operetta, in which the pet dog Dingo might just as well vote on behalf of the whole family." It is hardly surprising that he became a hero of the younger generation, saying out loud what they felt but did not yet have the confidence to articulate. Before long he was arguing for an end to one-party rule.

A week before the Soviet-led invasion on the night from 20th to 21st August 1968 he wrote a text arguing why it could never happen – that the Soviet Union would lose face and that its Warsaw Pact allies would never be willing to join in. Lenka Procházková recalls that one of the first things he did on hearing that tanks had crossed the border was to tear up the text he was in the middle of writing and try – unsuccessfully – to flush it down the toilet, a scene that has immediate echoes in *Ear*. For Procházka, as for the great majority of his compatriots, the invasion came as a deep shock, but it did not break him. Unlike many of those who had played an active role in the Prague Spring, he decided not to leave Czechoslovakia, and unlike many of those who stayed, he refused to acknowledge the official narrative of the invasion as "fraternal assistance". "We may have lost hope," he observed, "but we must not let them notice it." Over the coming months, he continued working on several screenplays, and he wrote *Ear* in the space of just three weeks of feverish hard work. He was under ever closer surveillance from the secret police as Czechoslovakia slid into the period known euphemistically as "normalisation", a drip-by-drip return to hard-line rule.

On 16th January 1969 the twenty-year-old student Jan Palach doused himself with petrol and set himself alight at the top of Prague's Wenceslas Square in protest against a creeping return to censorship and growing public acceptance of the invasion. In the days that followed Procházka commented: "I think that Jan Palach's sacrifice might really succeed in slowing down or stopping our growing tendency towards collaboration. Above all in its worst form – apathy. Of course, it is the romantic act of a young person. I fear that an older person would rationalise everything and no longer be capable of such an act. We would use countless excuses to persuade ourselves that it made no sense." Eight years earlier, at the end of the story *Lenka*, Procházka had compared the impulsive and courageous twelve-year-old heroine to Joan of Arc, and here we see him again, refusing to distance himself from the impulsive and romantic idealism of the young. Lenka Procházková remembers that there was always something of the child in her father and this inoculated him against any form of cynicism.

Remarkably, Procházka and Kachyňa were given the go-ahead to make the film *Ear*, and it was completed just before the end of 1969. It tells the story of one night in the life of a deputy minister and his wife, in the wake of the minister's arrest during the purges of the early 1950s. It is a perfectly crafted domestic political drama, a suffocatingly dark Hitchcockian thriller bordering on horror, with brilliant performances by Radek Brzobohatý and Jiřina Bohdalová as Ludvík and Anna, terrified that they are the next in line. Procházka and Kachyňa knew from the start which actors they wanted in the two roles, and Procházka was able to write the screenplay with both in mind.

As a study of the impact of surveillance, intimidation, fear and uncertainty on the individual, the film takes the pulse of its time, a fact that was to seal its fate. It was shown only once to an audience of a few dozen at the Barrandov studios. Lenka Procházková remembers that when the lights went up there was complete silence. No one clapped and just a few were brave enough to shake hands with her father. Everyone knew that the film would be unacceptable to the censors and would be banned before it even reached the cinemas. The screenplay had a similar fate, although it was eventually published in 1976 in an exile edition in Cologne.

The secret police launched an unprecedented campaign against Procházka that was to set the tone for their tactics of bullying and humiliating writers and dissidents over the next twenty years. They had made secret – and illegal – recordings of private meetings between Procházka and the writer and philosopher Václav Černý, during which Procházka had openly criticised some of the politicians of the time. These conversations became the centrepiece of a television documentary, broadcast in April 1970, carefully edited to discredit Procházka to the maximum. Paradoxically, for a writer who had spent years giving a voice to people who would usually find themselves marginalised, he was portrayed as arrogant and condescending, detached from the people. The documentary was followed by damning articles in the press. Procházka wrote letter after letter to defend himself, but he had no chance against a systematic, state-sponsored campaign. One of the most prominent literary figures of the Prague Spring, Procházka's fellow-writer Ludvík Vaculík, wrote to the Chief Prosecutor, protesting against the blatant violation of the law in broadcasting the recordings. He referred indirectly to Orwell's *1984*, but his words could just as easily be applied to *Ear*: "If you do not intervene to stop this, we shall soon find the nightmare utopia of the novel coming true, with people living like insects under a magnifying glass, monitored by the microphones and cameras of anonymous, untouchable and unaccountable usurpers." His letter remained unanswered.

Shortly afterwards, Jan Procházka was diagnosed with colon cancer. Had he not been in hospital, he would have been arrested in July 1970, in one of the waves of secret police arrests of people who continued to criticise the occupation. Police records show that they suspected him of feigning the illness and tried to have him transferred to the prison hospital in Ruzyně. He was able to spend Christmas at home, but his condition was worsening and he died on 20th February 1971, aged forty-two. The secret police tried to prevent the funeral from taking place in Prague, afraid that it could become a rallying point, and when that failed, they made a point of compiling a complete list of those who were present. The darkest period of normalisation was beginning, and from that moment onwards the choice was clear: keep silent or become a pariah in the eyes of the state.

Ten years after his death, his daughter Lenka remembers moving out of the flat where the family had lived in the Prague district of Hanspaulka. She warned the new tenants that they might come across listening devices from her father's time. "They called us back to say they'd found twelve, including the bathroom, the toilet and the balcony." *Ear* had not exaggerated.

In the end *Ear* was to outlive its censors. There was huge excitement when the film was first shown in Prague's Lucerna cinema in January 1990, just weeks after the Velvet Revolution. Shortly afterwards the book was published for the first time in Czechoslovakia. In the same year the film was nominated for a Palme d'Or at Cannes. Both the book and the film were seen not just as examples of the very best of 1960s writing and cinema, but also as a metaphor for the Czech experience of the twentieth century. Unlike many parts of Europe, this country was not devastated by war. It experienced instead a particularly insidious form of totalitarian rule, first under Nazi Germany and then as a satellite of Soviet Russia. At first sight, life went on as usual. By making certain compromises people hoped to get by, although at regular intervals they would be expected to humiliate themselves by demonstrating their loyalty in public. Sometimes the rules would change – suddenly and arbitrarily – as we see at the beginning of *Ear,* when Anna and Ludvík find out that Ludvík's boss has been arrested but have no idea why. Keeping people in a state of constant uncertainty is a tried and tested means of control. At the same time *Ear* shows how the regime was able to permeate every intimate corner of the private sphere. There is literally nowhere in the house where Anna and Ludvík can escape the "ear". Their private sphere no longer exists, but part of their tragedy lies in that they are fully aware that they have no right to complain. They have been compromised and have become complicit in the crimes of the regime.

For readers unfamiliar with Czechoslovak history, a few details in *Ear* need explaining. There are references to Edvard Beneš, the last pre-communist President of Czechoslovakia who died in 1948 just months after the communist takeover. The country's first President Tomáš Garrigue Masaryk is also mentioned. Both names, closely associated with the pre-war democratic First Czechoslovak Republic, would have been taboo in 1950s Czechoslovakia and then once again after the 1968 invasion. Just by mentioning them in connection with her husband, Anna is potentially compromising Ludvík's career in the communist hierarchy. Equally dangerous are references to Anna's middle class roots as the daughter of a publican. The good communist is expected at least to pretend to have a working-class background. At one point Anna and Ludvík argue about the financial difficulties they were in just before the communist takeover. By embracing the "revolution" in 1948, they found a convenient way of wiping out their old debts. Like many people in the 1950s, they were motivated to toe the line by opportunism rather than idealism. On two occasions *Ear* refers to politicians who have changed their surnames. This is a reminder that in 1950s Czechoslovakia, just as in the Soviet Union, people with Jewish-sounding names were looked on with suspicion. In the anti-Semitic show trials of the early 1950s, many prominent Jewish politicians were persecuted, regardless of their loyalty to the regime. Several were executed.

By showing in vivid detail how the system works, Procházka's book hollows it out and exposes its cruelty and cynicism, as it turns its victims into collaborators and its collaborators into victims. *Ear* could not have been written at any other time, but its context provides the framework for a psychological drama that is universal. The book is a deeply empathetic, but unflinchingly forensic study of the way people behave when placed under intolerable stress. We may not like Anna and Ludvík, but Procházka does not offer us the luxury of looking down on them. We know that we would probably behave in a similar way. That is the brilliance of this book. Anna and Ludvík are "only human", but so too are the forces that torture them, and in that way the cycle is perpetuated.

David Vaughan

Note: The author wishes to thank Lenka Procházková for providing helpful information during an interview, conducted in Spring 2022.

Trying to translate *Ucho* involved difficult decisions, not the least of which concerned finding the most appropriate title. In the end the most literal one seemed the best – the overpowering presence of the listening ear that is so all-embracing that it can even shave off the articles English uses to hold nouns in check.

The pace of the work and the dramatic form meant cutting grammatical corners to avoid weighing the text down. A relatively short book moves through eighty chapters from scene to scene, and the translator doesn't want to find himself holding the text back. I also felt that pace and immediacy required the present tense in most cases, with a reversion to the past tense sufficiently unusual to stand out.

There was also the translator's nightmare of language piled upon language, as visiting Russian dignitaries stumble over drink and Czech. It is for readers to judge how well this has been dealt with. As ever, however, this would not have been a translation at all without the help of others. Lucie Johnová suggested many, many improvements. My murderously meticulous wife, Lenka Zdráhalová, went through the text with her usual razor-sharp determination. Many thanks to them and also to the editor, Martin Janeček, for his helpful suggestions and delicate overseeing of the whole process through times of lockdown.

MODERN CZECH CLASSICS

Published titles
Zdeněk Jirotka: *Saturnin* (2003, 2005, 2009, 2013; pb 2016)
Vladislav Vančura: *Summer of Caprice* (2006; pb 2016)
Karel Poláček: *We Were a Handful* (2007; pb 2016)
Bohumil Hrabal: *Pirouettes on a Postage Stamp* (2008)
Karel Michal: *Everyday Spooks* (2008)
Eduard Bass: *The Chattertooth Eleven* (2009)
Jaroslav Hašek: *Behind the Lines: Bugulma and Other Stories* (2012; pb 2016)
Bohumil Hrabal: *Rambling On* (2014; pb 2016)
Ladislav Fuks: *Of Mice and Mooshaber* (2014)
Josef Jedlička: *Midway upon the Journey of Our Life* (2016)
Jaroslav Durych: *God's Rainbow* (2016)
Ladislav Fuks: *The Cremator* (2016)
Bohuslav Reynek: *The Well at Morning* (2017)
Viktor Dyk: *The Pied Piper* (2017)
Jiří R. Pick: *Society for the Prevention of Cruelty to Animals* (2018)
**Views from the Inside: Czech Underground Literature and Culture
(1948–1989)*, ed. M. Machovec (2018)
Ladislav Grosman: *The Shop on Main Street* (2019)
Bohumil Hrabal: *Why I Write? The Early Prose from 1945 to 1952* (2019)
*Jiří Pelán: *Bohumil Hrabal: A Full-length Portrait* (2019)
*Martin Machovec: *Writing Underground* (2019)
Ludvík Vaculík: *A Czech Dreambook* (2019)
Jaroslav Kvapil: *Rusalka* (2020)
Jiří Weil: *Lamentation for 77,297 Victims* (2021)
Vladislav Vančura: *Ploughshares into Swords* (2021)
Siegfried Kapper: *Tales from the Prague Ghetto* (2022)
Jan Zábrana: *The Lesser Histories* (2022)

Forthcoming
Ivan M. Jirous: *End of the World. Poetry and Prose*
Jan Čep: *Common Rue*
Jiří Weil: *Moscow – Border*
Libuše Moníková: *Verklärte Nacht*

*Scholarship

MODERN SLOVAK CLASSICS

Published titles
Ján Johanides: *But Crimes Do Punish* (2022)

Forthcoming
Ján Rozner: *Sedem dní do pohrebu*